TAMING THE STAR RUNNER

TAMING THE STAR RUNNER

S. E. HINTON

Delacorte Press

Published by
Delacorte Press
The Bantam Doubleday Dell Publishing Group, Inc.
666 Fifth Avenue
New York, New York 10103

Library of Congress Cataloging in Publication Data

Hinton, S. E.
  Taming the star runner / by S. E. Hinton.
    p.   cm.
  Summary: Sent to live with his uncle after a violent
confrontation with his stepfather, sixteen-year-old Travis,
an aspiring writer, finds life in a small Oklahoma town
confining until he meets an eighteen-year-old horse
trainer named Casey.
  ISBN 0-440-50058-3
  [1. Authorship—Fiction.   2. Horses—Fiction.]   I. Title.
PZ7.H5976Tam   1988   88-7065
[Fic]—dc19   CIP
                                                    AC

Manufactured in the United States of America

October 1988

10 9 8 7 6 5 4 3 2 1

BG

To Nicholas David

Acknowledgments

I'd like to thank my friend and typist, Dorothy Scott, for the courage to tackle my handwriting. I'd also like to thank my trainer, Libby Barrow, for her technical advice, which I always take in the ring, and sometimes took in this book.

TAMING THE STAR RUNNER

Chapter 1

His boot felt empty without his knife in it. It didn't matter that he had never had to use it (sure, he'd pulled it a couple of times to show off, but the times he could have really used it, he'd forgotten about it and used his fists, as usual); he was used to feeling it there, next to his leg. What a security blanket. But even if the juvenile authorities hadn't taken it, it wouldn't have made it through the airport scanner. I could have packed it, though, he thought.

Travis stopped at the end of the line of people waiting to go through the airport security check. The sight of the security guards made his heart speed up. It was already pounding out a rhythm a rock group could have used. He tucked the cardboard carton he was carrying under one arm and wiped the sweat off his face.

"No jokes," he said. Joe and Kirk looked at him blankly. They had been treating him funny since he got out of juvenile hall. Travis thought: They think I'm crazy like everybody else does.

Travis pointed to the sign. "No jokes about bombs and hijacking and stuff."

Motorboat meowed, protesting being held sideways, and Travis straightened up the cardboard box. Motorboat had been drugged at the vet's before they left for the airport. Jeez, he gets drugs and I don't. I'm the one who needs them.

He handed the box containing his cat to the attendant and walked through the detecting doorway, half expecting to set off an alarm. No alarm went off, and he picked up his box on the other side. Kirk, who had been to the airport before, didn't think it was any big deal to get scanned, but Joe was almost as nervous as Travis, and had to bite his tongue to keep from cracking a joke.

Joe would have been a great comedian in juvenile hall, Travis thought, since his reaction to tension was to get funnier and funnier, the way I get quiet and mean.

He couldn't remember ever seeing Kirk tense. Kirk could shrug his shoulders and walk out from under anything. He wondered for a second how two guys so different could be his best friends.

Mom was last. They had walked too fast for her to keep up with them. That was partly accidental. Travis could not slow down for any reason. It was also partly on purpose, because he couldn't stand any more of her soft frettings.

About how he should act when he got to his uncle's. About how he should stay out of trouble. (I could stay out of trouble all right, if it just didn't come looking for me. This last business sure wasn't my damn fault.) If it wasn't a mistake taking Motorboat with him. Like Travis should leave him here for Stan to kick around.

If he had packed the right clothes.

That last almost drove him to punch his fist through the wall. (He had done that once before —no bones were broken.) The right goddamn clothes! Sometimes he thought she was going to drive him crazy. He couldn't believe the stuff she had packed. New stuff (slacks, for God's sake!), stuff he'd shoot himself before he'd wear. Cowboy shirts! Could you believe that? He didn't care if Uncle Ken lived on a horse ranch. T-shirts were good enough to wear on a horse ranch. The horses wouldn't care.

Travis had dumped out all the new clothes and hidden them under his bed, and filled the two suitcases with his jeans and T-shirts and books and tapes and tape player. He wanted to take the tape player on board with him, but there was a rule about only one piece of carry-on stuff. He had learned a lot about the rules, trying to get the damn cat on.

It was practically a three-mile hike to get to the right gate, and they outdistanced Mom again.

There weren't too many people there yet, they
were way too early. Mom had seen to that. Not
that he minded. He couldn't take staying in the
house, now. He sure couldn't take any more time
in juvenile hall. What was left but leaving?

The plane was there, at the end of a long pas-
senger ramp. He could see it out the window that
took up a whole wall. It looked huge. The passen-
ger ramp looked like a giant eel, clamped onto its
head. God, that was a big plane! He'd never realized how big planes were. How the hell did they
ever get off the ground?

Kirk settled into a seat in the lounge. Kirk liked
to be comfortable. It was one of his biggest goals
in life. Travis set the cat carrier in Kirk's lap.

"I'm goin' for some cigarettes."

"This thing going to pee on me?"

"It'll improve your smell if he does. Come on,
Joe."

Travis and Joe strode down the hallway. Travis
had spotted the cigarette machine from a long
way off. He had left his at home and who knows,
maybe nobody on the plane would let him bum
one. Bumming cigarettes was one of his worst
habits. Travis knew that. He pretty much knew
what his worst habits were. Bumming cigarettes.
Getting into fights. A lot of times he drank too
much. On the other hand, he didn't bully anyone,
and didn't have a smart mouth like Kirk, and he
only bummed cigarettes, not money like Joe. He
wasn't a bad person, no matter what Stan was

saying. There were a lot worse people than he was.

They stopped at the john. Travis knew there were johns on the plane, but he wasn't taking any chances. Maybe he'd be sitting next to the window and have to crawl over a bunch of people to get out.

Next to the window. His breath stopped. Maybe not.

Travis combed his hair, staring into the mirror with fixed concentration. He was good-looking. Probably one of the best-looking guys in the school. He had dark brown hair, not so long that he looked like one of the dopers, not so short that he looked like one of the straights, the student-council preppies. Five foot eight. Not bad for sixteen, and by the size of his hands and feet he hadn't stopped growing yet. Good eyes. Great eyes, actually. Gray-green and as cold as the Irish sea. He had read a book about F. Scott Fitzgerald once, and it said he had eyes as cold as the Irish sea. Travis liked that. He secretly liked his eyelashes, too, a black fringe, as long as a girl's. He had a good build, long-boned and lean and flat-stomached, and that was the reason he liked tight T-shirts. Kirk was taller, and had broader shoulders, but Travis thought his own build was as good as any in the school. A lot of girls thought so. A lot.

"Maybe I'll get a tan," he said out loud. If he had a fault to find with his face, it was its paleness.

But then, from what he read, Fitzgerald had never tanned either.

"Huh?" Joe said. He never spent as much time looking in mirrors as Travis did, being one olive-brown color all over, hair, eyes, and skin, and inclined to pudginess.

"I'll probably get a tan, being outside all the time. You got any downers on you, man?"

"Hell, no. You think I'm going to try to go through that security shit with downers on me?"

"They're just looking for metal junk, like knives and guns. You could have brought some, they'd never catch it."

"Yeah? Then why didn't you bring some?"

"They weren't exactly dishing it out like candy in jail."

Travis knew the difference between jail and juvenile hall (it hadn't been so long ago that he was thanking God for the difference), but he liked to think that nobody else did.

Travis leaned forward . . . that couldn't be the beginning of a zit—he never got zits, except a couple on his back once in a while. . . .

"Trav—"

"Yeah?"

"Were you aiming to kill him?"

Hell, no, Travis thought. You think I want to end up in prison, getting gang-banged by a bunch of degenerates every day? You think I haven't got better ways to spend my life than dickering my ass for cigarettes?

"If I had wanted to kill him," Travis said, giving his hair one last run-through, "he'd be dead, wouldn't he?"

He was lying. He had meant to kill Stan, it was only a lucky accident that he hadn't. Now, the red rage gone and just the usual smoldering embers of hate licking at his insides, it seemed incredible that he'd trade his life (which wasn't any great shakes so far, but still, he liked it) for the chance of slamming Stan's brains out; that after the years of putting up with Stan, of taking belts and insults and beatings (even Travis knew the difference between a couple of swats and a beating), he would risk everything (which wasn't a lot, but something: music and hanging out and girls and above all that thing inside that said Travis is Special), blow it all for a chance to put Stan away forever. And Stan hadn't so much as laid a finger on him.

Stan was his stepfather. That didn't bother him. A lot of kids had stepfathers—in fact, he only knew three guys who had the same father they'd started out with. Stan had slapped Mom around a couple of times—that had bothered Travis when he was younger, but he liked to think it didn't bother him so much now. She could leave. Anytime. A lot of women worked. She wanted to put up with that garbage, she could. And not only did she put up with it, she kept making excuses for him. Like: "It was my fault, I shouldn't have been nagging. He is a good provider."

Provide, hell. Food on the table wasn't exactly living in luxury. Travis didn't think he wanted much, material stuff, anyway. Maybe a car someday, and all the paperback books he wanted, and tapes, tons of tapes until he could play tapes all night for a year and never hear the same thing twice unless he wanted; that wasn't a whole awful lot to want, really, but he sure as hell wasn't expecting anyone to provide it. He wouldn't let anyone provide it, a matter of fact. People give you something, then you owe them. Every time Stan bought Mom something, like an electric skillet or a new coat, just some simple little thing like you'd expect a guy to get for his wife, he'd beat her over the head with it. Not literally. But verbally. Like "I got you this and this and you owe me."

Getting beaten up verbally was just as bad as physically, only it was easier to hide the scars. Travis would never owe anybody anything. If he wanted something, he'd get it on his own.

Besides, it bugged the hell out of Stan that Travis never asked for anything. But asking for something put Stan in control, so Travis either got it on his own or he went without. He washed cars. He mowed lawns. He was the best poker player in the school. He worked at the vet's on Saturdays, or he had until he got fired for coming in late. Travis was hung over a lot on Saturdays.

But he got his own music and his own books and he could always take anything Stan dished out and walk off.

It was really weird to think he'd almost liked Stan once. When he was ten and Stan first started coming around—he'd been dumb enough at first to almost like him.

Just because he'd tossed a football around with him a couple of times, and promised to take him hunting. He cringed, now, to think how little he'd minded Mom marrying that creep, how he'd even halfway thought it was a good idea.

Stan was Mom's husband but he sure wasn't his dad; and he sure as hell wasn't his boss, and the older he got, the more Stan tried to . . . own him, Travis thought. That was the only word for it. Own him and try to make him sit up and beg. Well, Travis wasn't jumping through hoops for anyone. He went his own way.

Until last week.

Travis couldn't remember when he'd first known he was going to be a writer. He'd known as soon as he'd learned how to read, and he couldn't remember not being able to read. He had started in grade school, writing down the monster stories he'd make up for his friends. Spending the night with each other, hanging out in somebody's basement, sleeping on cots in somebody's backyard, Travis would tell monster stories, taking things he'd heard or read and mixing them up with what might be until he had it as real as reality—they'd all get scared (even Travis) and pick fights with each other or leave a flashlight on or get so loud that the grown-ups came after them, anything to get protection while denying they needed it.

Travis always had stories going in his head. From those monster stories to that long, involved tale he'd been telling his cellmate last week, he couldn't stop the stories any more than he could stop breathing.

He'd taught himself to type in the sixth grade. By then he'd realized that if he couldn't read his own handwriting, nobody else could either; he'd swiped Mom's Valium and sold it to a ninth-grader and bought a used typewriter. He liked the way his stuff looked, typed. Realer. More professional. By the time he took typing at school, in the tenth grade, he was typing ninety words a minute. That was the easiest A he'd ever made. In fact, the only A he'd made since grade school. He hadn't been such a wild kid in grade school.

It sort of puzzled him a little, being able to type. Most of the time he was damn clumsy with his hands. He wasn't any good tinkering with cars, the way a lot of his friends were, he was a real embarrassment on the basketball court. In shop class he had damn near cut off his thumb. You could take it for granted that he was going to drop or spill just about anything he had in his hands. But at a typewriter he just had to think and there were the words.

Stan disliked him for a lot of reasons. He was living proof Mom had had another husband. Travis was young and good-looking, he could take getting slugged across the face without changing expression; Stan's steady stream of gripes and cuts and digs only left marks where Stan couldn't see them.

Just a couple of months ago he had stomped into Travis's room, hauled him up from the typewriter, yanked him into the front room, and shoved him in front of the TV, shouting, "You're part of this family and you'll act like it."

Travis stared at the TV for two hours, writing a short story in his head, and typed it up later. Stan was not going to ruin it for him. He wasn't going to drive him to run away—Travis had seen what happened to the jerks who ran away, thinking something, someone, was going to fix things up for them—most of the time they came straggling home looking like idiots and when they didn't they mostly ended up in worse places than they were running from.

Stan wasn't going to drive him to suicide either. Sure, Travis sometimes thought about it. Everybody thought about it. It had been close sometimes. Once he had sat in an alley with a loaded .22 pistol and looked at it for a long time. But he hadn't put the barrel to his head. So it hadn't been *real* close. But he had thought about it. What had stopped him was his motto. His saying. What he told himself over and over again, like a prayer, a chant: He's not going to ruin it for me. He's not going to ruin it for me. He's not worth ruining it for me.

But last week, he damn near had.

It was an ordinary day. Travis went to school, tried to get a date with a new girl in class (she turned him down, nice girls usually did, because of his reputation; it had happened too often to bug him much). He had made a B on an English test (there was a note on it saying it would have been a A if he would learn to pay attention to spelling). He got into a shoving match with a senior out in the hall that just missed turning into a fight, and he cut history after lunch to keep on cruising with Kirk in his Firebird, listening to a new tape. It was a real ordinary day. . . .

Then Kirk dropped him off at the house and he walked in to find Stan stuffing the fireplace with something. Stan just glanced at him. "I've heard your mother tell you a thousand times to clean your room. Now I'm cleaning it for you."

Then Travis realized the papers were his stories, his songs, stuff he had spend years writing.

Later, he tried to recall what had crossed his mind, but he couldn't remember a thing but the red blinding explosion that didn't seem to take place in his head at all, but was triggered somewhere between his gut and his heart.

And then Stan was lying on his side, keeled over like a beached ship, still clutching a wad of paper. Blood was starting to trickle down to his face from his scalp. Travis was staring at the fire poker he held tight, with both hands, like it was a baseball bat.

The rest was a jumbled mess. Mom crying and calling an ambulance and neighbors running in—Mrs. Landell saying, "You have *got* to do something about that boy!" in a tone of voice that made Travis want to smash her too. The bitch.

(She was always complaining about Travis: He played his music too loud, his light stayed on all night, keeping her awake, all those hoody friends hanging out in the driveway, laughing, drinking beer, up to no good, their tires squealing out at odd hours.)

When the cops showed up a few hours later, Travis was sure that was Mrs. Lendell's doing. But no. It was Stan who had signed the complaint. . . .

They really did read you your rights, just like on TV. Travis had been close to laughing, it was so much like TV. But the cold steel of the handcuffs wasn't like TV. Travis had been shocked at how it felt to be handcuffed and dragged out to the police car. Embarrassed. Not angry or defiant or a little pleased with the stir he was causing in the neighborhood. He had imagined being arrested before, for some daredevil, spectacular crime that would get him on the six o'clock news. He'd never dreamed that the main thing he'd feel would be just plain humiliated . . . and really, really scared.

"We better be getting back," Joe said.

Travis knew that sometimes he made Joe very

nervous. Joe probably suspected Travis was, like people were saying, a little bit crazy.

Okay, Travis thought. So what? Writers were supposed to be a little bit crazy.

"Yeah. In a minute," Travis said automatically. He shook himself slightly, like a dog rising from a nap. "You gonna write me a letter, man?" He ripped open his cigarettes and jammed one in his mouth, sticking the pack into the pocket of his brown leather jacket. Joe handed him a match-book.

"Sure. I guess." Joe had never written anyone a letter in his life, he wasn't making any promises.

"Really, I want to know how things are going. What's happening—"

"Travis, we'd better be getting back, you're gonna miss your plane . . . what's wrong?"

Travis closed his eyes for a second. This was why he had wanted Joe to go with him, not Kirk. Joe wouldn't care. What was better, he wouldn't blab, he could tell Joe—

"I'm scared."

Joe looked at him uneasily. "Hey, listen, your uncle's probably a pretty good dude, he's got to be better than—"

"Not my uncle, man, I'm scared of the plane. I'm scared to get on the goddamn plane."

The plane. How could anything that big . . . it must weigh tons, how could it leave the ground, much less stay up there? Who was driving? Did they know what they were doing? It wasn't easy,

driving a plane . . . what if they were hung over
or flirting with a flight attendant or something?
Just careless for a couple of minutes, then what? A
fall, straight down, minutes of knowing what was
coming . . . Travis broke out in a cold sweat.
And he was expected to just bop on in and hand
over his life to strangers.

"You ain't scared."

Travis slumped back against the wall and met
Joe's eyes for a second. Joe was appalled. Travis
Harris, the coolest, the toughest . . .

"Remember that drag race we had with those
guys from Central?" Joe asked.

Of course, Travis remembered it clearly. They
were in the twins' Trans Am and Travis was driving. He was the only person they let drive their
car. He was doing 110 on the expressway and he
took one hand off the wheel to take Kirk's beer
and slug it down, his other arm trembling with the
effort of driving, and everyone was holding his
breath. He hit 115 and nobody was breathing at
all, and he asked for another and Billy—maybe
Mike—gave him one quickly, afraid he'd turn
around and take it. They were flying, skimming
the road, the Central guys left behind long ago,
and nobody, man, nobody thought he'd get the
car back down. He just kept on asking for more,
faster, harder, they couldn't even hear the radio
anymore or see the lights rushing by in the night,
as if they were all suspended in time, nothing real

except the lights on the dashboard where the nee-
dle kept climbing. . . .

"Remember that, Trav? You can't be scared."

Travis stared down at his boots. "I was driving."

Back at the gate, Kirk had put the cat carrier on
the seat next to him, and three little kids were
gathered around trying to peer in the air holes.
Kirk was telling them it was a baby leopard. "No
kiddin'."

Mom started to get up, then sank back. "You
need to go to the counter. For seat selection—
they'll give you a number. Here, take the ticket."

She hadn't trusted him with the ticket. Travis
was notorious for losing things; it was the major
reason he was always bumming cigarettes. His
just disappeared.

More lines. Smoking section. Aisle seat. He'd
have to go in the smoking section anyway, because of Motorboat. A boarding pass. Something
else to worry about losing.

Travis went back to his seat and picked up Motorboat. "Hey, kid, get outta here. Leave the cat
alone, huh?"

Travis wasn't crazy about little kids. Anyway,
M.B. was probably having a nice downer, he
didn't need a bunch of brats messing it up for
him.

They all sat there in silence, like they were waiting for the movie to start. Travis kept on smoking, one foot bobbing to music only he could hear.

"When you comin' back?" Kirk said.

Travis didn't reply. Sometimes when he did this it was because he was out of it (he referred to his habit of blanking out, visiting some other world that was always spinning in the back of his mind, as "being out of it"; it rarely happened when he was drunk), or it was because he chose not to answer. Most people couldn't tell which was which. Travis found this very convenient.

"Next summer," Mom said. "Travis will proba-bly be home next summer."

"Wow, that's a long time, man."

The authentic note of distress in Kirk's voice made Travis glance at him. He had never made up his mind about Kirk—Joe was his friend because he was Travis. But he had the feeling that Kirk was his friend only because he was one of the coolest guys in the school. The cool guys always hung out with each other. He liked Kirk's smart mouth, and even though he was good-looking in a big butter-scotch Viking kind of way, it was the kind of good-looking that wasn't competition. A matter of fact, they looked good together. But Travis found it hard to believe Kirk would actually *miss* him.

"Write me a letter," Travis said.

"Yeah, and you'll put it in your book."

"The book's finished," Travis said. He didn't add that weeks ago it was in the mail to a pub-lisher. Nobody needed to know that.

"Yeah? Am I in it?"

"Yeah. The comic relief. Say bye to Billy and Mike for me."

The twins worked at McDonald's and couldn't get off. There could have been quite a crowd here, saying good-bye to Travis.

Travis cut the conversation off. He didn't talk about his writing. Joe and Kirk were the only guys who knew why Travis would hole up for days in his room, the music blaring, not cruising, not hanging out, missing dances and parties and fights—the rumors about this ranged from "heavy doping" to "really weird." Travis didn't care what they said. He honestly never gave a damn what people said about him—or at least, what they were saying about his frequent disappearances. The writing was just so much a part of him that he couldn't talk about it any more than he'd sit around and spill out his guts. It was nobody's business.

"Those people in rows ten through twenty-one can be seated now. Please have your boarding pass ready for the flight attendant. No smoking beyond the gate."

Travis dropped his cigarette and stamped it out. A crowd surged at the gate, people hugging and calling good-bye to each other. He got up, the cat carrier under his arm. He looked at the waiting plane; his heart jumped. "Geez," he muttered, "how do they ever stay up?"

Kirk said, "Angel dust."

Mom was giving him a lot of last-minute instructions and messages and lectures. Travis couldn't hear any of it—not that he wanted to—the plane crowded out every other thought in his head.

He shook hands with Joe and Kirk. Kirk surely noticed how cold and sweaty his hand was. Maybe he'd tell the other guys. Travis was a real chicken-shit about flying.

Maybe not.

Mom was standing there. Travis suddenly hugged her, even though he hadn't been planning to. She was sending him away, she had chosen Stan over him a long time ago . . . she had never understood the slightest thing about *Travis,* she loved him, sure, blindly, because he was her kid, it didn't have anything to do with *him.* . . . Travis was shocked to find tears jumping to his eyes.

"See ya," he said, turning.

"Be good, hon."

"Yeah, sure."

He followed the other passengers down the long hall. Somebody took his boarding pass and gave him a piece of it back, somebody told him where his seat was. The line stopped, people grabbed for a magazine, or stopped to put their coats in an overhead rack, holding everyone up. Travis found it hard to breathe. There didn't seem to be a lot of air in here.

He found his seat. Next to the aisle, not the

window, thank God. "Store all carry-ons safely.
. . ." a voice was saying.

He got his seat belt fastened. A blast of air was
hitting him from somewhere. He wondered if the
plane had sprung a leak. The engines started up.
"In case of emergency . . ."

He strained to hear her, but no one else was
paying attention, the engines got louder, his heart
thudded until he thought he was going to throw
up. The babbling voices around him had a hollow
sound, a chorus of the damned.

The plane backed out with a sudden jerk. They
were moving. Slowly now, cornering, then faster,
faster, a lunge—his stomach jumped. God! The
ground was gone!

"Is that a cat or a dog?"

Travis slowly dragged his eyes from the window
to the man sitting next to it. Surely they weren't
supposed to be tilting like this, the ground
stretched out beneath them . . . a long, long
way down. . . .

Travis glanced at Motorboat's box, stored
safely beneath the seat in front of him, just like the
attendant had said. "Cat."

The engines changed noises. Man, that
couldn't be right! Something was wrong. What
was that weird grinding sound beneath them?
Travis's hands were ice-cold. The armrests under
his gripping palms were wet. Sweat ran down his
back. And still they were going up. . . .

"I hate cats."

Travis looked at the businessman, who was thumbing through an airplane magazine. And beyond him, the window. Where there was nothing.

I'm going to black out, he thought dizzily. Then he took a deep breath. No way.

He reached nonchalantly for his own magazine.

"Yeah, well, I hear a lot of faggots hate cats."

He stared without reading, the engines humming in his head.

There was nothing left but leaving.

Chapter 2

Dear Joe,
It's okay here. My uncle seems to be okay. I started school. It's real small. Everything is okay.

Travis broke off typing. Great literary merit in this letter, all right. What if someday, after he was famous, somebody published all the letters he'd ever written? Sometimes they did that with famous-author letters.

He'd sure be proud of this one. He yanked it out of his typewriter and rolled in a new page.

Joe—
I lived thru the plane ride even tho we had to stop twice on the way. I thought I'd puke all over the dude sitting next to me, and it woulda served him right—I

tried to get him to buy me a bourbon but he wouldn't go for it.

My uncle is younger than I thought he was, people seem to think we look alike and I'm not real insulted, except he has some gray hair. He recognized me right away at the airport.

Travis stopped. When he'd asked Ken how he had recognized him, he'd replied, "That last-of-the-cowboys swagger, just like Tim's."

And there'd been something in his voice that Travis couldn't place; bitterness or regret or both. . . .

I guess I must look like my dad. Anyway, Ken's separated from his wife, they're going to get a divorce or something. We're living out in the country, I think he was raising horses but doesn't anymore, he said he didn't have the time since he was made a partner in his law firm. That *might come in real handy, huh? (ha ha)*

He's a funny kind of dude, I haven't figured him out yet. Real quiet, and sometimes it takes me a while to get what he's saying, because he says funny stuff with a real straight face. Like I tried to say thanks, for letting me move in like this, and he said, "I wanted to do something nice for a change. . . ."

Travis leaned back. He had the feeling his uncle didn't quite know why he'd let him come here.

They still seemed to feel funny around each other, like they were both thinking: Now what?

But Ken left him alone and Travis was happy to be left alone instead of griped at. He didn't even mind how quiet it was around here.

I go to this little hick school out in the boonies—I got sent to the office the first day for saying "goddamn." Can you believe it? The kids are such aggie-nerds it is totally unbelievable—

"Let's go get a pizza."

Travis looked up at his uncle.

"Or maybe you need to finish your homework?"

Travis shook his head. "Naw. It's just a letter."

"You writing your mom?"

Good grief! Writing to Mom, what an idea. What the hell could he write to Mom?

"Naw, I'm up for pizza."

Actually, one of the best things about this setup so far was pizza. Ken liked it as much as Travis, although he loaded his half with a bunch of junk like green peppers and mushrooms, when just plain cheese was the way pizza was meant to be.

Travis stared out the car window.

It sure got dark out in the country. It was two miles to the Pizza Hut, a mile and a half to the nearest 7-Eleven. He was thinking he needed a job, but it sure wasn't going to be easy, getting around. He didn't think Ken would be crazy about either letting him drive, or driving him around. He had made it pretty clear that Travis would ride the bus to school.

"Uncle Ken?" he began, but his mind got sidetracked when Ken answered, "Yes, nephew Travis?"

"Why do you do that, call me nephew Travis? You want me to drop the uncle bit?"

"You got it."

"Okay." Travis had felt like a dork every time Ken called him "nephew Travis" but wasn't sure if it was supposed to be funny or what. So far, he was trying real hard not to get Ken ticked off at him. It was weird, living with a stranger. But probably, he reminded himself, a whole lot better than living with a bunch of strangers. A really strange bunch of strangers. . . .

He glanced around the almost-empty Pizza Hut, so glad he was here and not in jail. . . . There were three girls at a table in the corner and one of them was pretty.

He hadn't made any friends here yet, not having found anyone he particularly wanted to be friends with, and suddenly he wanted to talk to somebody his own age.

He looked at the girls again. The pretty one and the fat one were listening to the third girl. She leaned over the table, talking eagerly, waving a cigarette toward an ashtray and missing.

Good excuse. It'd worked before. He left Ken ordering the drinks and walked up to their table.

"Hey." He made eye contact with the pretty one; she smiled politely and glanced away. He turned to the third. "Can I borrow a cigarette?"

"Here." The girl who had been talking slapped a dollar bill on the table. "Go buy yourself a pack."

She went on with her story, as if there hadn't been an interruption. Travis stood there stupidly, trying to think of his next move. He'd used this ploy a lot; get a cigarette, get a light, keep talking. Not just with girls, but with anybody who seemed interesting, who might have a story. . . . Nobody had ever thrown a dollar at him and told him to get lost.

"Casey"—Ken came up and handed Travis a Coke and sipped the foam off his beer—"you meet my nephew, Travis? This is Casey Kencaide, who leases my barn. Jennifer—"

The pretty one said hi.

"And Robyn."

The fat one said hi.

"How'd the show go?" Ken went on.

"Pretty good," Casey said. Her eyes were interesting, green as traffic lights. Actually, if she'd had on some makeup and a different hairstyle, she might not have been so plain. Profile a little too severe, and way too skinny. . . . Jennifer was cute, though. *Real* cute.

"We pinned in almost every class and Jenna got small hunter champion."

"How'd the Star Runner do?"

"Well, we made it to the jump-off."

The thing that saved her face, Travis thought, besides those vivid eyes, was its expression: not quite laughing, a light smile at a private joke. But she was too old for him anyway, at least eighteen.

"Then he crashed through the triple," Robyn said. "He had the whole course down."

Jennifer said, "Not the *whole* course."

"Number nineteen, your order is ready," said the loudspeaker.

"That's us," Ken said. "See you, girls."

"Yeah, see you," Travis echoed.

Casey said, "Ken, up his allowance. He's bumming cigarettes."

Just got back from pizza with my uncle, Travis began typing again. Motorboat jumped up in his lap and put his chin in the crook of Travis's elbow; Travis couldn't see how the cat could be comfortable— as he typed, Motorboat's head jarred up and down until his teeth clicked together. But he always did this while Travis typed, purring loudly and doing happy feet, his needle-sharp claws lightly spiking through Travis's jeans.

How's it going there? Weren't you and the twins going to work for Orson? They ever get the transmission fixed on the Trans Am? Done any cruising lately?

Travis stopped, and took a deep breath. He was starting to sound homesick. Couldn't start sounding homesick.

Anyway, he wasn't homesick. There wasn't anything at home, especially. Nothing to be lonesome for. Hanging around watching the twins fiddle with their car, or spending evenings in the parking lot of the city park, sipping beers until the cops ran you off, what was so great about that? Messing around in Orson's record store after school, listening to his line of bull—he was always hinting around that he was involved in mysterious Big Deals that someday, if they were real lucky, he'd let them in on. He said he knew the Mob. He also said he owned the record store, when Travis knew for a fact he just managed it. And he had a strong suspicion that the mysterious Big Deals went on mostly in Orson's head.

He was one of those older guys who seemed to think they were still young. That always irritated Travis. Being young was an exclusive club and pretenders annoyed him.

And Orson kind of gave him the creeps. But then, Travis never had to particularly like someone to find them interesting.

But still, it was kind of a kick to hang out in the record store, you got to hear a lot of new releases, and Travis couldn't feel bad about lying to Orson, he was such a liar himself, so it was a good place to tell stories. A lot of the heavy dopers hung out there, so there might have been dealing going on, but Joe and the twins and most of Travis's friends weren't druggies, so it wasn't done in front of their faces. Maybe the twins bought grass.

Mom called. I guess Stan isn't permanently brain damaged. Not that he'd know the difference. She said you guys were having a lot of rain lately. No tornadoes here yet, but at school there's a drill. . . .

Great. Talking about the weather—how dumb. Probably because people around here talked about it more, which showed you how desperate they were for conversation—weather at home was just something that made the difference between sitting *in* the car at the park, or *on* it.

Disgusted, Travis pushed back from the typewriter and Motorboat jumped down. The cat raced around the room, his tail stuck straight up, pausing to grab Travis's leg, biting, thumping hard with his hind legs.

"Okay, okay." Travis kicked loose. "I'll let you out tomorrow."

He hadn't let Motorboat out of the house yet, afraid he'd get lost. But maybe he'd try it for an hour or so tomorrow. He'd have to be careful; Ken had a couple of dogs and might not like them getting beaten up by a cat. He read his new Hemingway biography for an hour, then wandered down to the den where Ken was looking over a bunch of legal papers and watching the news at the same time.

He looked up, and Travis felt for a minute that Ken had forgotten who he was and what he was doing here. He'd felt that before. It made him really wonder why Ken had let him come in the first place.

"Finish your schoolwork?"

Ken asked him that every night. It was like it was the one safe conversation piece.

"Yeah." He hadn't, but he could do it on the bus in the morning. "Can I have a beer?"

"No."

"I drink it at home."

"You're not home."

"Yeah, but—"

Ken put his papers down. "Subject is closed, kid. I don't have the energy for this kind of garbage. You want to drink beer, go home."

"Yeah, okay, no big deal." Travis figured he'd just sneak down later for a swig of bourbon.

"You doin' legal stuff?"

"Yeah, I'll shuffle these papers around awhile, then I'll give them to someone else to shuffle and when enough people have shuffled for the appropriate time, something of no lasting value will be decided."

"I thought being a law partner was a pretty good job."

"Being a partner is fine. It's the practice of law that sucks."

Travis wandered around the room, picking up stuff and looking at the pictures on the wall. Most of them were of a chubby blond baby growing into a chubby blond little boy. Ken's son Christopher—would that make him his nephew, cousin . . . ?

"Ken?"

"Yeah."

"How old are you?"

"Thirty-seven."

Travis was shocked. "Oh, wow, man, you don't look that old."

"Thanks." Ken's voice seemed even drier than normal.

"Can I ask you something?" Travis was talking almost absentmindedly. It was a good thing he'd brought a lot of books with him, there didn't seem to be many here.

"I'm betting you can."

"Huh?"

"Yes, you may ask me something."

"Oh." Travis dropped into an armchair, fiddled with a lever, and almost flipped himself over backward. When he got straightened up he said, "Was my dad some kind of gung-ho Rambo, joining the Air Force to whip the commies?"

His dad had been shot down over Vietnam two months before he was born. Travis was curious about him. Mom always spoke of him as a "good man and a brave soldier," but Travis couldn't tell much from that. Not that she'd have the story straight anyway. She tended to remember things the way she *wanted* them to have happened, instead of the way they did.

Not that it had much to do with him. He didn't have a dad, but neither did a lot of people. No big deal.

"No," Ken said slowly. "Not at first. But he got more and more militant, got so bad, in fact, that we couldn't carry on a conversation for five minutes without getting into a fight. . . . No, at first he just wanted so bad to fly—"

Travis got up abruptly. He didn't want to hear about flying right now. And Ken seemed glad to change the subject.

"Kid."

"Yeah?"

"Change the cat's litter box."

Stan had griped a lot about that too.

"I'm goin' to start lettin' him out tomorrow— he'll whip your dogs."

"They won't bother him. They're used to cats."

"Yeah?" Travis was interested, "You got a cat?"

"I had a cat. Teresa's got custody."

Travis wandered back to his room. Maybe Ken was so preoccupied because of this divorce deal. Well, it probably was rough, but you had to admit, it wasn't anywhere near as bad as attempted murder.

Chapter 3

The whole world had turned on him! Travis didn't get it. Nothing was happening the way he wanted it.

Ken was too distracted to pay much attention to him, but Travis hadn't expected an open-arms welcome, and who knows what Ken had expected.

No, Ken was okay, it was school. The other kids. Travis was easily the coolest guy in the school. That was apparent the first day. He didn't see anyone worth hanging out with. They all talked so weird, slowly, dragging out every word with a drawl too hokey to be real.

He was sure the first day that this was all an elaborate put-on for his benefit. Just a joke on a new kid. He was stunned and amused to find out the truth—people really talked like this! And they moved so slowly, his own movements made him look like a speed freak. They even ate lunch slowly.

After the first week it was a little less noticeable, at least enough to keep him from laughing out loud. But by then he wasn't much in the mood for laughing, anyway.

It was starting to dawn on Travis that these people didn't seem to realize how cool he was, much, much cooler than anyone else in this hick school—you'd think people would be standing in line to suck up to him. But it wasn't happening.

There wasn't any group for him. Back home there were lots of different groups. He could even comfortably drift with two or three. Here it was just hicks. Hick jocks and hick nerds, maybe. He didn't fit.

He preferred Trans Ams to pickups, speed to four-wheel drive. He liked hard rock instead of country. His language shocked even the boys. The girls worth looking at were looking at somebody else. He felt weird, moving so much faster than everyone; when he tried to slow down he became clumsier than ever. Getting into trouble for his foul mouth, he tried to curb it and couldn't —the solution seemed to be keeping his mouth shut. Nobody wanted to speak to him anyway.

His English teacher was not impressed by his first theme. The first page was covered with red corrections. At the top of the second she'd written, *I give up! Buy a dictionary.*

A **D** on an English paper in a school where they
barely spoke English!

Well, he'd lived before with teachers who
weren't madly in love with him. He could handle
that. But he'd never been without friends.

He remembered feeling sorry for new kids at
his old school, not that he ever went out of his way
to make their lives easier. At least he didn't tor-
ment them, like Kirk had.

In fact, in the eighth grade, he went out of his
way to get the twins into his group, figuring twins
might be interesting; he hadn't known any before.

They weren't particularly, but Travis didn't regret befriending them.

They had transferred from another school in
the middle of the school year when their parents
got divorced; maybe that accounted for their
stunned and rabbity-looking faces. Skinny, blond,
never quite clean, dressed alike in plain T-shirts
and jeans, Travis got to where he could tell Billy
from Mike when he saw them together, but didn't
know whether he was speaking to Billy or Mike
when he bumped into one of them alone. They
rarely were alone, though, it made them uneasy—
all their mother had to do to keep them in line was
threaten to send one to live with their father.

No, Travis never regretted including them,
though once the novelty of their being twins wore
off they weren't anything outstanding. And when
their mother remarried, their stepfather would
buy them grass.

Interesting or not, Travis would have given anything to have them over for an evening, or better yet, gone to hang out with them while they flipped burgers for McDonald's, because on top of everything else, he was starving.

> *Joe—*
> *This place is okay except there's nothing to eat. Really. Remember how you guys thought I was absent-minded? Well, you should see my uncle. He keeps forgetting I'm here—he works late a lot and eats a sandwich at the office and I'm stuck out here in the middle of nowhere with no wheels and an empty fridge. So Ken comes in at nine o'clock and does a double take at finding someone else here and swears and off we go to the 7-Eleven for a microwaved barbecue beef. . . .*

Mom would croak if she knew how he had to scrounge around this big old house trying to find something edible. Mom was a good cook, you had to give her that. The memories of the dinners she used to fix could almost make him cry. Macaroni and cheese and pork chops and potato pancakes and fried chicken—homemade desserts every night.

He hated to admit it, but he was sick of pizza.

> *Listen, Joe, it sounds funny, but the other night I got desperate enough to try to cook spaghetti. The directions say "cook till tender." How am I supposed to know when that is? Anyway, it came out kind of chewy and*

the only thing I could find to put on it was a can of
tomato soup. Ken came in and found me eating that
stuff and we drove clear into town to an all-nite
Safeway and we stocked up on frozen dinners and lunch
meat so at least I'm set for a while. You'd think Ken'd
realize somebody's living here by now. . . .

Travis got up and wandered down to the den,
where Ken sat in front of a *Star Trek* rerun working
on papers. It was hard to keep on writing Joe
letters when he didn't write back—Travis had
known he wouldn't, but still, it was like putting a
note in a bottle and tossing it out to sea. Actually,
it was hard to write anything these days.

Here was the perfect time to hole up in his
room and write, but his mind seemed as blank as a
typing sheet. Maybe because it wasn't his choice,
anymore, now that there was nothing else to do.

"How's school?" Ken asked automatically.
Usually, Travis said, "Okay," and that was their
evening conversation. But tonight Travis said,
"Rotten."

Ken looked up.

"Really. Nobody likes me."

"I like you."

"Yeah, but you don't go to my school."

Ken laughed and put down his papers. "Okay.
Listen, hang in there a little while longer and if it
doesn't get any better I'll get you transferred to
East River. It's a lot bigger, there'd probably be
somebody who'd like you."

Travis didn't see anything funny about this, and it might have shown on his face, because Ken said, "Just try it a little longer, okay? I've got a heavy caseload right now, and this thing with Teresa's on my mind—"

Great, thought Travis. Ask him to spend two minutes on my problems and we're back to his. . . . "You're not being a farmer anymore?"

"Rancher. No. At one point I was going to be a gentleman rancher, which I found out is impossible. Unless you're fantastically wealthy and unbelievably sane, you can't ranch in your spare time. Fortunately, I got out before the bottom dropped out of the market . . . Teresa was bored out here anyway. . . ."

Why would he care if she was bored? They were divorcing.

"There's nobody to hang out with," Travis said, getting back to the main problem.

"The barn is swarming with girls every afternoon. Some of them are pretty cute. Hang out with them."

Hang out with girls! Now he could believe Ken's remark about not being totally sane. The idea was too dumb to even discuss. All he said was, "I don't think what's-her-name, Casey, likes me."

"Unless you're on a horse, or *are* a horse, she's not going to like you. You sure seem to worry a lot about being liked."

For the first time Ken had really ticked him off.

Travis had never, in his whole total life, given a damn about being liked. Who cared? Who gave a— He got up off the floor and went outside. He hated *Star Trek* reruns. Mom was a Trekkie. She even made Stan take her to the *Star Trek* movies.

He sat on the short wall of the patio. Except for the purple glow of the bug zapper, it was pitch-black. It got so dark out here. . . . Motorboat jumped up and walked along the wall. Travis held out a fist and the cat shoved his face against it, then the top of his head, rumbling loudly.

After a while, Travis went to spit in the bug zapper, to hear it zit.

It was invisible-man time again at school the next day. Even the big hulk who'd gone out of his way to harass him the first week had given it up, like it wasn't worth the bother. Travis remembered a kid at his old school, a real loner who was suspected of being a psycho, and for the first time wondered if that kid had really *wanted* to be a loner. If maybe somehow all the other kids had forced him into it, without even being really aware of what they were doing. He'd always assumed that being a loner was something you chose—now he knew other people could choose it for you.

Okay, so this was the way it was. He kept up his swagger and answered his teachers in monosyllables; he spent lunch smoking in an empty corner of the baseball field or in the library. He kept a faint sneer on his face, even while combing his hair in the john, noticing miserably how round his ears were, like teddy-bear ears, how pale his face. These damn suckers were making him doubt his looks.

He went down to the barn after school. Not to hang out. Just to see what was going on. . . .

Casey gave riding lessons after school and on weekends; she was at the barn to feed and water before he caught the bus in the mornings. He'd gone down to the barn before, carefully waiting until her Jeep was gone, to look at the horses. Now he was going to look at the girls. . . .

Casey stood in the middle of the ring, four little girls on ponies trotting in a circle around her. As each one went by she barked an order: "Molly, get your heels down. Amber, get your leg back, your leg should be on the fat part of the horse. Megan, you're posting too high. Wrong diagonal, Liz."

Travis folded his arms on the top rail of the ring and watched. God, it was hot. It'd be a lot cooler at home by now. Here the heat just sat on you, like a cloud. The riders looked even hotter, with all that hot junk they had to wear—boots and pants and hats. Casey was wearing shorts and a T-shirt and a sun visor, and she didn't look too cool either.

"When you get to the brush box, canter."

Only one little girl managed what he assumed was a canter. The rest of the ponies just trotted faster.

"Don't throw yourself forward! Sit up! Pull up and try it again. Get organized."

Travis had thought about learning to ride, but he'd thought Ken could teach him. All this flitting around in an English saddle looked too la-di-da for him. Besides that, he hadn't seen anyone except girls doing it.

"Hi. You ever get any cigarettes?"

Travis had seen Jennifer coming up behind him, but had pretended not to, deciding to let her speak first.

"Yeah, I did. You riding today?"

Jennifer really was cute, dark hair in an expensive-looking short cut, dark eyes. She was wearing tight gray riding breeches, high boots, and a polo shirt.

"I'm in the next lesson. I've got to go tack up in a minute. Casey," she called, "Robyn won't be here, she had to stay after school."

Casey left the circle of riders. Dust had settled like a tan across her face, streaked here and there by little rivers of sweat.

"What?"

"Robyn got in trouble, she had to stay after for a conference with her mother."

"Great." She kept an eye on the riders and suddenly yelled, "Molly, don't let him walk off with you like that! You should have pulled him up after the first step!"

She turned back to Jennifer. "Robyn was going

to do the stalls for me. I've got a horse-show meeting this evening!"

"I'd do it," Jennifer offered, "but I've got my piano lesson right after this."

"You. Nephew. What's your name?"

"Travis." He was annoyed by her tone—sure, maybe she was a *little* older, but not that much.

"Would you do something for me? I've got to split after this next class. Would you go up and water the stalls for me?"

Her green eyes were a much warmer color than his own. They saved her face from plainness. Too bad, he thought, she had to go and ruin her nice long legs. They were way too muscled up.

"Yeah, sure," he said. "Okay."

"What a pal," she said, and went back to her students.

"How old is she?" he asked Jennifer as they walked back to the barn together.

"Casey? Eighteen, I think. She's the youngest pro in the state."

"You like her?"

"Oh, sure, I mean, she's a real perfectionist, she makes you work real hard, but we do win ribbons at shows. I'm a little bit scared of her."

I can see that, Travis thought, but sounded surprised as he said, "Scared?"

"Oh, not scared, but you know, she's so good and I'm such a klutz—I fell off right in front of the judge last time. I thought I was going to die."

"What'd Casey do?"

"Came out and gave me a leg up."

Seeing his puzzled look, she added, "Boosted me back on and told me to finish the course."

There were two girls in the barn, getting their horses ready to ride, and one older lady, thirty at least.

The girls were too young to be interesting, probably around thirteen. They looked enough alike to be sisters, blond and freckled, though one had a bad perm. And from the way they acted, they could have been twins. Unlike the pair back home, they were loudmouthed and silly, shrieking, "Oh, Kristen!" "Oh, Kelsey!" at each other, and in ten minutes they were driving him nuts. He thought they might be driving the older lady nuts, too, because she got her horse saddled and out of there, fast.

Travis watched Jennifer brush and fly-spray her small brown horse. He liked the part when she cleaned its feet with a pick, because it called for a lot of bending over.

Kristen and Kelsey were ready first and the barn was much more peaceful. They'd been gone about ten minutes by the time Jennifer had her saddle and bridle on, and Travis was surprised to see her near tears.

"If my lesson runs late Mom'll kill me. I've got to go straight to piano from here. Oh, damn."

She led the horse out of the barn at a trot, and almost ran down the red dirt road toward the ring.

The little girls from the first class were riding into the pasture behind the ring. He decided he'd get the stalls watered and be back in the house before they got back. Little girls didn't interest him.

The work didn't take long.

He stopped halfway in the kitchen door. There was a blond woman in the kitchen. She looked too well dressed to be a burglar, but Travis froze a minute anyway. . . .

She paused, too, then relaxed. But she was staring at him as if she were seeing a ghost.

"You must be Travis," she said finally. "God, you look more like Ken than Christopher does. I'm Teresa," she added.

Teresa, Ken's wife, or soon-to-be ex-wife. Boy, she was good-looking—but he always had been a sucker for brown-eyed blondes. What was Ken divorcing her for? Then he remembered: she was divorcing him. Immediately he was on Ken's side.

"I guess I mean you look like Tim. I never did meet him, but in their pictures they look quite a bit alike."

"Yeah." Travis could remember only one picture of his dad, in his Air Force uniform; he remembered the eyebrows, especially, being like his, almost joined in the middle. Stan had made Mom put it away. But frankly, he didn't see this big resemblance to Ken everyone else did. "But he's premature gray."

"He's premature thirty-seven," Teresa said dryly.

Travis gave her a look that let her know whose side he was on, and she changed the subject. "I brought Christopher out. I'm going out of town tonight on business and I knew Ken wouldn't mind getting him a little early. I tried calling him at the office but he was out."

Christopher. The little kid. He seemed to remember Ken saying something about the little kid coming out this weekend, but he hadn't been paying attention. He thought of something: He'd been planning to nag Ken into doing *something* this weekend, even if it was just going to a movie. Now they wouldn't be going anywhere more exciting than a Dairy Queen.

"I will say this," Teresa went on, "—Ken gets an A-plus in the daddy department. That's so important for a boy—" She broke off suddenly and, in a voice trying too hard to be pleasant, asked, "Now, what was it you got in trouble for? It wasn't drugs, was it?"

Travis had it on the tip of his tongue to answer, "No, it was attempted murder."

But something made him change it to "Oh, my stepdad and I don't get along too good, Mom wanted us to chill out for a while."

"Yeah, broken families are the pits, aren't they?" She stopped to examine a nail. Poor lady was having a hard time finding a polite subject.

"You want to meet Christopher? He's up in his room making sure all his toys are still there."

"Uh, I got a lot of homework, I thought I'd get started on it."

He just wanted out of there.

"Sure. You guys will have plenty of time to get together this weekend."

I bet, Travis thought sourly in his room, throwing himself across the bed, turning his radio up. He'd never been around a little kid and was positive it was going to be a real pain.

All the damn radio stations sucked.

At home, he'd be hanging around the record store, maybe he and Kirk would be planning to pick up some girls. . . .

He gave up on the radio and slammed in a tape and turned over on his stomach. Motorboat was walking up and down on his back, his happy feet pricking holes in his shirt—he had ruined a lot of Travis's shirts.

At home, he'd be cruising to this music, or sitting around the front porch with four or five guys, somebody would be peeling out down the street, whooping out a car window as they passed.

He lit a cigarette, remembering well enough he'd promised Ken not to smoke in bed, but it wasn't like he was *sleeping* or something.

At home there'd be people to talk to, whether it was the most outlandish lies or absolute truths or both in the same sentence. . . .

Something tickled his nose and he was startled to find it was a tear.

There was a light knock on his door. Quickly he sat up and brushed his face off.

"Yeah?"

"Travis, there's someone here to see you."

Travis, completely puzzled, opened his door.

"Casey's in the front hallway," Teresa said, and added, "Good God. That cat is huge! Is he, uh, gentle?"

Travis glanced down. Motorboat's head was level with his knee.

"Yeah," he said absently. "Sort of."

Teresa didn't seem too reassured, but Travis couldn't care right now.

Why would Casey want to see him? He'd thought she had some big meeting to go to.

She was waiting patiently in the entry hall, and Travis thought suddenly that if she were a boy, with that angular profile and long-distance gaze, she might be sort of good-looking.

When she turned that gaze on him, however, he could have sworn it was with a mixture of laughter, anger, and contempt. He shifted uneasily in silence, finally saying, "Yeah?"

"Are you an idiot?" she asked, pleasantly, as if she were asking, "Are you a Leo?"

"What?"

"I mean, are you brain damaged or what? Ken didn't mention it, and I didn't think to ask."

"What?"

"What did I ask you to do this afternoon?"

Travis had a sudden flashback: He was eleven years old and absentmindedly made lemonade with six *cups* instead of six *tablespoons* of sugar. . . . Stan had had a really good laugh about that one. . . . What a stupid thing to think about, right now. . . .

"Water the stalls," he answered. He could tell something horrible was coming, he'd look up and see a freight train on top of him and there wouldn't be time to move.

Casey nodded. "So that's what you did. Watered the stalls."

They stood there for a moment under the hall light, and it seemed like all this had happened before, that they had played this scene in a play a dozen times before, he could even tell her next line:

"You are an idiot."

And as Travis realized the mistake he'd made, he couldn't even argue with her. A slow wave of heat spread upward and he knew he was bright red.

"Now I've got ten stalls inches deep in water. Couldn't you figure out I meant put water in the buckets—not all over the floor? Good golly, kid, are you brainless?"

Travis thought later he should have slugged her. How could he have stood there and taken that?

Probably because at the time he agreed with her and couldn't even get the air to say so.

"I bet," Casey said slowly, "that when your mama asks you to tie your shoes, you rope them to the bed."

Travis stood there a long time after she closed the door behind her.

He wasn't cool. He wasn't tough. He wasn't even good-looking. He just stood there, a brainless, homesick idiot.

Chapter 4

Dear Travis: Every thing is OK hear. The Twins got Fired for comin in stoned so me and them are doin stuff for Orson. NOT DEALING. Kirk is going preppie. It make you sick. He is even dating Lisa Mahoney. Hows it goin.

Joe

A short letter, but a lot to think about. Travis wished he had the twins here, so he could knock their heads together. He knew it. He knew the minute he left town, they'd turn into dopers. Here he'd gone to a lot of trouble to get them into his group, get them some friends because they were too shy to get their own, and they knew how he felt about heavy doping.

Billy and Mike weren't book smart, but in their

field, mechanics, they were damn geniuses. Travis was awed by the way they could take things apart, put things together. They had a ticket there, and they were going to blow it.

Fired. How were they going to pay their car insurance? And the three of them, Joe included, were idiots for "doin stuff" for Orson.

You'd better get paid in cash, up front, guys, he thought.

Kirk going preppy, huh? Travis, looking back, could see it coming; he had noticed last summer when Kirk gave up cutoffs and sneakers for Jams and loafers. No, that didn't surprise him at all. He'd known all along Kirk planned on college— he'd never tried to hide his good grades, like Travis sometimes had.

Not that there was anything to hide, now.

"How's it going?" Well, Travis thought, I'm hanging out with an uncle, a little kid, and a bunch of girls. It is just going super.

He could still hang out with the girls. He'd followed Casey down to the barn and silently taken the shovel and wheelbarrow and helped clean up the stalls.

In return she'd told people the water pump had broken.

It'd been one of the hardest things he'd ever had to do, but if he hadn't he'd never go to the barn again, and he had to have *somewhere*.

He wasn't sure yet how he felt about the little kid. Christopher was a big pain, just as he'd expected. But there was something kind of interesting about someone who just said and did whatever came to mind without worrying about it.

Christopher was the roundest person Travis had ever seen. His chubby face was round. His big brown eyes were round. His blond haircut was round. His chunky little legs and arms were round.

And his round mouth moved constantly.

"Well, hi." He crawled up into Travis's bed early Saturday. A lot earlier Saturday than Travis liked.

"Are you sleeping?"

"Yeah."

"Why?"

" 'Cause I'm sleepy."

"Why?"

" 'Cause it's early."

"Why?"

In a very short time Travis thought he'd freak out at the sound of that word.

Christopher was exact. If you failed to say please, thank you, or you're welcome, he'd correct you. If you called something by the wrong name, he'd correct you. "It's not a cuckoo clock. It's a bird clock."

You couldn't have a sandwich or a Coke to yourself. You had to share. He was real big on sharing. And it was a little disconcerting to be around someone you didn't know too well who didn't hesitate to crawl all over you.

Christopher poked into everything, messing up his tapes, drawing on his papers. And Motorboat, who had stared down Ken's Labrador and slapped the chow's nose the first day he was out of the house, spent the weekend cowering under the bed or behind the sofa.

But Ken seemed to think everything Christopher did was cute, and took it for granted that everything revolved around him. He jumped when Christopher said, "More juice please," scrubbed his hands before every meal, and when Christopher waddled bare assed into the den with his underwear around his ankles and announced, "I did poo, come see," Ken reacted like it was a miracle.

Hell, thought Travis, it'd be more of a miracle if he didn't do any.

He hated to admit it, but maybe he was just a little bit jealous.

He watched Ken answer the phone and try to talk with Christopher climbing up his back, hanging around his neck, yelling, "I will fall you down!" and laughing till Ken couldn't hear or make himself heard; Travis marveled at his patience. He'd have pitched the kid across the room by now. . . .

"It's for you," Ken repeated, holding out the phone, and Travis shook himself awake. Who'd be calling him?

He took the phone, grateful that Ken was hauling Chris out of the room.

"Hi, hon."

It was Mom. He remembered how he'd called her Donna the Hon, even to her face, and he was suddenly ashamed.

"Hi."

"How are you?"

"Okay."

"How's Kenny?"

"Okay."

"Everything fine?"

"Yeah. What's up?"

He couldn't bring himself to ask about Stan.

"I just wanted to make sure you were all right."

"Yeah." Surely she knew Ken would call her if he got run over by the school bus or something.

"Well, hon, are you getting enough to eat?"

"Sure," he lied a little; it was spooky that she'd ask that, though. . . .

"Travis, you've got a letter here from a publishing house—you haven't been buying a lot of books or joined a book club?"

"Naw." Travis thought for a minute. "No—wait! Don't open it!"

"What is it?"

"I don't know." He paced in a small circle, dragging the phone, tripping over the cord. "I don't know. Just send it to me, okay? Don't open it."

"All right, hon. I'll get it in the mail tomorrow."

"Tonight."

"What?"

"Get it in the mail tonight, okay?"

"Well, hon, by the time we get through with dinner I think the post office will be closed."

Let the big slug skip dinner for once, Travis thought, but knew that was impossible. He couldn't think. He couldn't talk.

"Hon? I've got to get off the phone now, I promised Stan I wouldn't talk too long."

"Put it in the mail right now," Travis said slowly.

"Say hi to Kenny for me. I wish I could see his little boy. Send me a picture, okay?"

"Don't open it."

"Bye, hon."

Travis had trouble getting the phone back on the cradle, weird damn phone, shaped like a doughnut.

The book! The book! He was going to hear about the book he'd written! He'd tried hard just to forget about it, knowing it'd be a long time before he heard anything, but it had nagged at him like a dull toothache.

That was probably why he hadn't been able to write lately, he thought suddenly, why he hadn't really written anything since he'd sent the manuscript off. It was like something unfinished. . . .

He expected a rejection. All writers got lots of rejections. Hemingway had gotten about a million of them. He wasn't sure how many Stephen King got.

It was okay, getting a rejection. You wanted to

write, you just had to get used to it, like if you wanted to fight you had to take getting punched. He'd just send it to another publishing house, he had the next three places picked out already. What he was hoping for, really, that whoever read it this time would tell him something, anything, it was too long or too short or too—whatever. Why they didn't want it—that was all he was hoping for, this time.

But maybe they did. Maybe they were saying, "We'll publish it and here's a million dollars!" He had a strong desire to call Mom back, have her open it and read it to him. He wasn't going to be able to stand it.

No, she didn't even know he'd written a book, much less sent it off. She knew he wrote, sure, but seemed to think it was some weird phase he was going through, though after all these years you'd think . . .

No, it was his book and his letter, no matter what it said. Nobody needed to know anything. Just him and somebody in New York. For a second he wondered who . . .

Ken was grilling hot dogs on the Jenn-Air.

"Anything up?"

"Naw." Travis wished Ken weren't such a hard ass about letting him drink anything. He sure could use a slug of bourbon. "She just wanted to make sure everything was okay. Was I eating right, you know."

"I hope you lied." Ken took the mustard knife away from Christopher, who was trying to mustard the hot dogs still on the grill.

"Yeah, I did." He remembered something. "She said to say hi. She called you Kenny, made you sound like a little kid."

"She always did—called Tim, Timmy too. He swore when he had a kid, the name'd be something she couldn't put a *y* on."

"I thought she picked my name."

"She did, but Tim had to approve it. He was sure you were going to be a boy. . . . She got the name out of a book, didn't she? The MacDonald mystery series?"

"No, *Old Yeller*. The dog book."

"Tim used to tease her about all the books she read."

Mom reading? He hadn't seen her read anything except *Reader's Digest* and *National Enquirer* and those books that always had a picture of a pirate ripping the shirt off some girl. That wasn't *real* reading.

"Your mom was a real sweet girl. Pretty too. She thought Tim hung the moon."

Hung the moon. What a weird expression. Travis had never heard it.

"She's fat now," Travis said. He tried to think of Mom young, pretty, and reading, and couldn't do it. Young, pretty, and reading and thinking someone hung the moon. . . . Obviously she thought a lot more of Stan than Travis could, but he wasn't any moon hanger.

"Come here," Ken said suddenly. He picked up Christopher and sat him on one of the high barstools at the center island table.

"Put your hand next to Chris's, open your fingers. See?"

Travis stared at the two hands, wondering . . . then he saw. Christopher's hand was a miniature of his own. The shape of the fingers, the set of the thumbs—Travis was startled to see even a lot of similarity in the palm prints.

"Wow."

"He's got Teresa's coloring and features, but my details: Ears, hands, feet."

"Let me see yours."

Again, an amazing resemblance. Travis thought: That's how my hand will look. But surely not that old.

"Do I remind you of my dad?"

"Just in looks. You're a lot quieter. Tim was a very . . . vivid personality."

"You guys get along?"

"Once a year."

"Why'd you let me come here?"

Ken met his eyes. Ken had light brown eyes, clear, like iced tea with the sun shining through.

"Why'd you want to come?"

And Travis knew exactly when the same thought went through both their minds: I thought you'd be Tim.

* * *

Federal Express, he thought, I should have told her to Federal-Express it. He couldn't eat, he'd hardly slept, and he couldn't expect the letter for two more days, anyway. It would have cost a lot of money, he wasn't sure how much, but he could have hocked his tape player—no, calm down, whatever the letter said it would say the same thing two days from now.

He went directly to the barn after he'd put in his time at school. The house was more peaceful, now that Christopher was gone, but Ken was in a bad mood. He was ticked off because Christopher had left saying a word he hadn't said before; Travis figured if Ken had cable TV like any normal person the kid would have said it long ago. Anyway, it was plain that returning Christopher to Teresa was what was really bothering him.

Anyway, it was fun down at the barn after the lessons, although the girls were sillier, louder, goofier, than any bunch of guys could be. And the second he walked in, they got sillier, louder, and goofier than ever. Kristen and Kelsey weren't twins, they just acted alike. Which meant they screamed a lot. Robyn had an incredible motor mouth (Travis realized that coke was at least partly to blame—she'd offered him a hit the second time he saw her), and Jennifer mostly giggled; to get her to squeal you only had to see—or pretend to see—a mouse.

Mary, the older lady, always left as soon as

she'd cooled off her horse, but unless there was a music, or ballet, or some other kind of lesson (Travis was amazed at how some days they absolutely ran from lesson to lesson), everybody hung around for a while.

Motorboat loved the barn. He'd spent a lot of his time there since the weekend—Christopher wasn't allowed in the barn. He lazed on the rafters or sat on a horse, doing happy paws—once in a while he brought out a mouse for Jennifer to squeal at.

Casey didn't seem to mind the noise, but usually she was too busy to add to it. She went straight to the little office–tack room. She kept an orderly record book—who had a lesson on what day, whose horse she was riding, vet records, horseshoe bills.

She either did that, or stopped down by the paddocks to stare at her big gray horse, the Star Runner. Everyone said the Star Runner was a mean dude—Travis hadn't seen Casey ride him, so all he could judge for himself was that the Star Runner was the only horse to have a paddock all to himself; he was the only horse who seemed to be constantly in motion, walking rapidly up and down, up and down.

Today Casey was in the office on the phone, oblivious to the noise.

"You know, you shouldn't smoke." Kristen had Charlie, her horse, untacked, ready to lead it out to the water pump for a shower. She paused beside Travis, then suddenly snatched his cigarette pack out of his T-shirt pocket.

"Come on, give 'em here."

"They're really bad for you." Kristen ducked to the other side of her horse, giggling.

Travis sighed. Now he'd have to go chase her around for a while, or give up his last pack. They weren't too easy to get around here.

"Give 'em here." He just straightened up off the wall, but Kristen shrieked as if he were lunging for her, and ran out of the barn with her horse trotting behind her.

"Hey, get back here," Travis shouted from the doorway. Damn dumb kid. He felt stupid having to chase her, and mad that she could make him do it.

Kristen grabbed the short mane of her horse and swung up. She used the lead rope for a bridle, dancing Charlie in a small circle. He snorted nervously.

"I'm going to throw them in the water tank and lengthen your life."

"Yeah, and you'll shorten yours. Get back here."

He took a step. Kristen screamed and kicked Charlie into a trot. It was muddy down by the water tank—all the pony kids had hosed their ponies off earlier.

She really is going to do it, the little jerk, Travis thought as he ran after her. As Kristen twisted around to throw the pack over the rail into the

water tank, the Star Runner, who had been trotting up and down at the far end of his paddock,
charged the gate. He made a horrible squealing
sound. With his head held low, swinging from
side to side, his ears pinned flat, he seemed to
Travis for a split second like some monstrous
snake. . . .

Kristen's horse scrambled sideways, lost his
footing in the mud, and fell with her. Then he
rolled to his feet, trotted a few yards, and began to
eat grass. Kristen lay still in the mud.

Well, she's dead, Travis thought, oddly detached, as he ran down the hill. She had to be,
he'd seen the horse roll on her. But he ran on,
hearing Jennifer scream, "Casey! Casey!"

She was alive, her eyes were open and she was
moving her lips. There was something wrong,
though. Even in his first quick relief he knew there
was something wrong. . . .

"Don't move." Casey knelt beside her, pressing
her back when she made a move to get up. How'd
she get here so fast? he wondered. How . . .
then he saw Kristen's leg, there was something
strange about the angle of her right leg, something weird sticking through her jeans. . . .

He shivered, suddenly sick.

"What's wrong?" Kristen's voice sounded very
young and breathless.

"What is it?"

"Your leg's broken," Casey said, "It's going to
be okay, a broken leg heals. Travis."

He tore his eyes away from the bloody white piece of bone. He thought he was going to puke.

"Go call an ambulance. Tell Jennifer to call Kristen's mom, and tell her we're going to St. Francis Hospital. You can call nine-one-one for the ambulance. Got it?"

"Yeah." Having something to do cleared his mind.

"Casey, it hurts." Kristen sounded astonished and a little miffed.

"Sure it hurts," Travis heard Casey reply as he started back to the barn at a run. "It's probably going to hurt worse in a minute."

He rushed past a white-faced Jennifer to call nine-one-one. He had a hard time remembering the address and the operator got a little sharp with him.

Jennifer flatly refused to call Kristen's mom, so he had to do that too. He could see why: Kristen's mom went into hysterics and it was obvious that would have sent Jennifer into them too.

He got the mom off the phone and on her way to the hospital, had Jennifer sitting quietly on a tack box whispering, "I can't handle this," told Robyn to take care of Kristen's horse, made Kelsey go home instead of hanging around getting in the way.

Then he grabbed a horse blanket to take down to Casey. He'd seen a wreck once, everybody was putting blankets on everybody.

Kristen was whimpering by now, and Travis

couldn't blame her, wanting to whimper himself every time he caught sight of her leg. Casey held her hand, talking quietly: "I know it hurts really bad, Kristen, but pretty soon you'll be at the hospital and they'll give you something: Just think, this time tomorrow it will barely hurt at all. Just hold on a little bit longer—"

It seemed more than a little bit longer to Travis by the time the ambulance arrived. Kristen screamed while they put her on the stretcher, and he thought he'd rather have the broken leg himself than be a helpless witness to it.

As the doors shut Casey said, "You know how many times I've told those kids not to fool around with the horses? I wish it'd been her goddamn neck."

Travis, almost shaking with reaction, could have slugged her. Then the lights and the siren went on, and the Star Runner, who'd been dancing up and down the far side of his paddock, took two giant strides across it and cleared the top rail. He also cleared Travis.

"Goddamn," Travis breathed. He ducked, seconds late. He watched the gray horse thunder down the pasture road, clear the gate, and disappear over the ridge.

"Goddamn."

"I knew he was going to do that," Casey said.

"Yeah? Well, thanks for the warning." Travis glanced at her. It could have been his neck—

Her head thrown back against the sky was a

thing to stop your heart. Transfixed like a saint by a vision, Casey watched the empty horizon.

Travis suddenly knew why they called it falling in love. It did feel like falling, helpless, half terror and half exhilaration. Wishing desperately to call it off, Travis, wishing it undone, calling it stupid, senseless, hopeless, everything but a mistake, knew he was in love.

"That sucker can jump, can't he?" Casey asked. The joyful intensity of her voice made his pulse leap.

"Yeah." He choked, kicking around in the mud for his cigarettes, not daring to look at her any longer.

He hadn't known it was going to feel like this.

It was going to take getting used to.

Chapter 5

. . . I think you have captured a certain spirit here very closely. . . .

It wasn't a rejection slip. He'd known it wasn't a rejection slip before he tore open the two envelopes. It was too long to be "We regret that your work doesn't meet our needs at present," or whatever a rejection slip said—he knew a rejection slip would be short and thin like a fortune in a cookie. This was a real letter, whatever it said; someone thought enough of the book to write him a real letter.

And flawed though it is, some of its flaws are as interesting as its virtues. I would like to speak to you personally about the possibility of publishing your work. . . .

That meant yes. They were going to publish it.

Travis still stood at the end of the driveway where the school bus had left him. He usually checked the mailbox anyway, it was a long hike down to the house and Ken had asked him to— Ken invariably forgot and had to go back for it. Travis had been surprised to find how eagerly he looked forward to the mail—even letters from Mom. But today he'd slipped his hand into the short silver tunnel gingerly, as though expecting a snake. . . .

I am going out of town for a few weeks and if possible, I'd like to visit you and discuss this with you. My number is 212-555-4200.

Sincerely
Eleanor Carmichael
Editor-in-Chief

Travis walked up to the house, unsure of what he'd read, the words that were used, but just about positive that they meant he was going to get published. He'd sold his book. He stopped on the front step to read it again. Yeah, that's what it said. Possibility, hell, some New York bigwig wasn't going to fly out here and "discuss" with him unless they were pretty damn serious!

Fly out here. They had his old address at home, not this one. He was a lot farther away now. Maybe she couldn't make it now!

He dialed the number and got an operator telling him to dial 1 before the area code. Hell, he'd never dialed long distance before, nobody'd ever told him that.

"Eleanor Carmichael's office," a voice announced.

"I want to talk to her, Eleanor Carmichael."

"Who's calling please?"

"Travis Harris. She wrote me a letter—"

"Just a moment."

Travis danced in a small circle, suddenly wishing he'd gone to the bathroom before calling.

"This is Eleanor Carmichael."

"Yeah. This is Travis Harris. I got your letter."

"I was wondering when I'd hear from you."

"I moved, I live in Oklahoma now, I just got the letter. Can you come out here?"

"If you're between New York and L.A. I can."

"Yeah, I think we are. Uh, Mrs. Carmichael, you going to publish it?"

"Ms."

"What?"

"Ms. Carmichael. Well, Travis, I'd like to speak to you in person. There're a few things I'd like to discuss. The profanity, for one thing, will severely limit the market—but as I said, I'd rather talk to you in person."

"Sure. Okay. But tell me, like I clean up the language and stuff, you'll probably publish it, right?"

There was a short sigh. "I should have known

from your novel . . . Yes, if we can agree on some revision, we'd like to publish it."

Travis remained silent, trying to understand. This was really happening. . . .

"I want you to understand, there's usually not a lot of money involved for a first novel—don't go out and buy a Porsche. But if we can get this to the right audience, I think word of mouth might be terrific. . . . Travis, are you still there?"

"Yeah."

"Have you told anyone?"

"There's nobody here to tell."

"Oh. Well, I'll write soon and let you know when I'll be there. Can I have your new address and phone?"

After he hung up he dialed Mom. She'd be nuts. He'd like to see the look on Stan's face. There was nobody home. He called Joe. He'd be nuts. There was nobody home. He called Ken at the office and his secretary said he was in a meeting. Travis was having trouble breathing. He walked around and around in circles.

Motorboat jumped up on the sofa and Travis grabbed him and shook him. "I sold my book! I sold my book!"

Motorboat twisted loose and ran.

He might as well tell Casey—she'd be down at the barn by now. He might as well tell her, she'd find out anyway.

He had to tell somebody.

Jennifer and Kelsey were hanging on the arena rails.

"Hey," he said. "Guess . . . What's going on?"

Casey was riding the Star Runner. He had never seen her ride him before. She was cantering him around in a small circle while a lady stood on the side.

"More inside leg, Case. You need more bend."

"What's going on?" he repeated. He kept looking at the Star Runner's face. He could swear it was seething with rage.

"Oh, look at that frame!" Kelsey sighed. "He's so beautiful."

Beautiful, yes. Breathtakingly beautiful—but for a second Travis had a cold, irrational fear: This was no flesh-and-blood animal at all, but something demonic. . . .

Casey sat deep in the saddle, using her whole body, back, legs, shoulders, to maintain that hold, her will against his will.

"Casey's taking a riding lesson?"

"Dressage," Jennifer said. "It's a real technical form of equitation."

"Good, Casey. Very good. Downward transition to a walk." The instructor dropped her voice as Casey came up to talk.

"I just don't see how Casey can stand it. He just hates all this. He's never going to love her."

Travis was remembering some of the stories he'd been hearing around the barn, about the

Star Runner, bits and pieces he hadn't paid much attention to before.

How he'd been a lunatic horse, practically given away off the racetrack, how he'd jump out of his paddock to race alone in the pasture. Casey's biggest fear was he'd kill himself running one of these hot days—he didn't know how to stop running. The kids wouldn't go near him. Only Robyn was brave enough, or stupid enough, or stoned enough, to groom him. He'd bitten one of the handlers at the track, tearing off a chunk of flesh —Casey herself had a scar on her forehead, he'd reared up on her while she was leading him. Casey, laughing, called it the mark of the beast.

"Don't be silly, Jenna," Kelsey was saying. "Casey doesn't care if he loves her."

Casey rode next to where they were standing, her face abstracted and intent.

"Casey, you don't care if the Star Runner loves you, right?" Kelsey asked.

Travis couldn't believe she had the nerve to break in on Casey's exhilaration. He knew the feeling. Like walking to the front step after a good chapter and finding the guys blithering about getting laid, getting drunk.

Casey didn't have time to connect to what she was saying before Kelsey went on, "You just want him to love jumping, right?"

Travis said, "She wants him to do it because he *can* do it."

Casey stared at him for a second, startled.

Okay, he thought, staring back, I do know you better than anyone else does. Think that over, lady.

He turned and walked off. He didn't want to tell her about the book right now. Jennifer and Kelsey would get silly excited, but Casey, right now, would say, "Yeah? That's great," or something offhand that would make him mad. He didn't want to be mad right now. He didn't want to be mad, and didn't want to hear that a damn dumb, crazy gray horse was more important than his book.

His book. He'd sold his book. For a few minutes there he'd been sidetracked, but it came flooding back over him now, and he knew what he wanted to do. Right now. As soon as he could.

He wanted to party till he puked.

He had never hitchhiked much at home, he hadn't needed to, his hangouts were in walking distance even if he hadn't had friends with wheels. And he didn't know anywhere to go, here.

He sipped a water-glass full of whiskey while he thought it over. Crown Royal was great, he decided, pouring a Coke-bottle full to take with him. It was just going to waste here; he'd never seen Ken drink anything more than a couple of beers.

He finished his glass with a couple of quick gulps. Hell, he'd just ask his ride where to go.

It was too hot for his leather jacket but he wore it anyway. He needed a place to stash his Coke bottle. Besides . . . besides, between the jacket, and the whiskey, and news about his book, he was starting to feel like his old self again.

He ended up on a really good street. That was the good news. There were several clubs with live music, a couple of packed restaurants, and the clientele seemed to be pretty upscale; it didn't look like he'd have to spend the evening worrying about getting jumped.

The bad news was, it looked like the only thing open to somebody his age was the Quik Trip. He had a fake ID, but it gave his age as eighteen, so it was no good here. He strolled up and down the street a few times, checking things out, making a game plan.

One club was so packed that people spilled out onto the parking lot and sidewalks, wandering around with drinks in their hands, laughing and yelling to each other. It was hard to tell exactly where the club began and ended. These people probably were twenty-one, but not much more than that; he didn't feel conspicuous at all, hanging around the edges.

He bummed a cigarette, asked about the band, kept an eye on the doorway where the IDs were being checked. It wasn't too long before he had a chance to slip in.

He played it cool, squeezing into the back of the crowd, staying away from the bartenders. He picked up an empty glass to pour his whiskey into; when one of the harried cocktail waitresses saw him, she assumed *someone* had checked his ID when he bought a drink. It looked like he was going to get away with it. He relaxed and surveyed the scene.

It was the worst possible place for live music. The acoustics were so bad it was like being in a tin cave, and unless you were right up front you couldn't even see the band. But the music didn't seem to be important.

People stood around in small groups and yelled in each other's ears, the guys checked out the chicks, the chicks looked the guys over, sometimes the two groups ran together. They all seemed incredibly dumb to Travis. But then, when he had been ten, teenagers had seemed incredibly dumb, and by the time he was twelve he was dying to be one—maybe it was going to be like that.

Right now he couldn't imagine giving up hanging out for this kind of scene.

He bummed a Virginia Slim from a couple of girls.

"You look awfully young to be in here." The redhead, in tight jeans, high heels, and T-shirt, kept wiggling around to the music. She obviously wanted to dance.

"I just turned twenty-one today," Travis said. "I'm celebrating."

"Really? All by yourself?"

"I'm new in town—just started law school."

God, it felt good, the whiskey, the music, the telling of a story; it was like he'd been walking in his sleep the whole time he'd been here, up till now.

"So you're a Virgo, huh?" The dark-haired girl was a little drunk.

"Do you know Jim Beals?" said the redhead. "He's in law school."

"I don't think so. I just started—you ever heard of Morris and Harris? That's my uncle's firm."

"Oh, yeah, I've heard of them."

"I wouldn't have thought you'd be a Virgo. I would have said Aquarius."

Travis almost jumped—he *was* an Aquarius. But he just shook his head.

"This is the first night I've been out since I moved to town. Any other good hangouts?"

They talked awhile longer—Travis trying to remember lawyer-type words he'd heard Ken use. The girls insisted on buying him a birthday drink —he went to the john when they called the waitress over. He'd never had a margarita before, it was pretty good stuff. They kept talking. When it was time for the next round he gave them the money for it and headed off for the john again. They probably thought he was tooting up or had the world's weakest bladder.

He got drunk enough to make a big mistake— he told them about his book. The dark-haired girl had been skeptical from the first, but he and the redhead had been having fun; now he lost them both.

"Oh, yeah, sure, you have a book coming out."

And when he kept insisting—dammit, he had to tell somebody—they started disbelieving *everything.* He knew exactly when it dawned on them he wasn't twenty-one either. He'd lapsed into talking like sixteen and couldn't stop it.

They finally said they were going to the ladies' room. Of course they had to go together. He spotted them twenty minutes later with some other guys.

So what? He found an empty chair at the back of the room, almost got into a fight over it—people were lurking like vultures to pounce on empty chairs.

He was in a crowd and still lonesome. It was as bad as school. He wished he'd told Casey after all, it would have been better than wasting it on those bimbos. He tried to picture Casey in this place. . . .

"Let's see your ID."

Travis looked up, startled. Some guy with a beard was glaring down at him.

Travis searched his pockets.

"Uh, I guess I lost it. Maybe in the john. I'll go see—"

The guy hauled him up by his jacket and shoved him toward the door.

The crowd had thinned out quite a bit, and Travis wondered what time it was.

"Gary, did you let this kid in here?"

They paused by the doorman.

"Hell, no."

Gary followed them outside. Travis assumed he was kicked out and was ready to go anyway, but the guy still had a grip on his jacket.

"He didn't come up through the drainpipes. How'd you get in here?" He shook Travis like a stray cat.

"Oh, you know, I walked—"

"You didn't walk by me, man," Gary said.

"Who sold you drinks?"

This is getting real boring, Travis thought.

"Look, I'm new in town, I didn't know what your drinking age is."

"It sure as hell ain't fifteen, man."

"I could lose my license over this, dammit! You know what kind of money I put in this place? What kind of money I *borrowed* to put in this place?"

He was shouting at Gary but shaking Travis, who was having a hard time standing up anyway.

"Who sold you drinks?"

"Nobody, really man, I brought my own. . . ." He searched through his jacket, then vaguely remembered he'd left the empty Coke bottle on a table.

"Look, nothing's happened—" Gary began.

"Something's happened all right—you're fired."

He finally let go of Travis and stormed back into the club. Gary and Travis stared at each other.

"And you're dead meat," Gary said, and

slugged him. Travis went down on his butt, then flipped backward and cracked his head on the parking lot.

It had been too long since he'd been in a fight, he decided. He'd forgotten how much it hurt to get punched.

"Get me fired, will you? I needed this job—"

Travis rolled to avoid getting kicked, got to his feet, and flew into Gary with a couple of swift jabs. He had the satisfaction of seeing both surprise and blood before getting knocked on his ass again. This time he wasn't fast enough to miss getting kicked.

If I wasn't drunk I could take him, he thought. Then: God, don't let me be killed before my book's published.

The owner came back out and pulled Gary away.

Travis lay there and listened to them yelling at each other.

At least it wasn't my nose, Travis thought, curled up around his cracked ribs like a worm on a stick. He coulda really ruined my face.

It was a while before he felt like moving. For one thing, he wanted to make sure both those guys were gone. He thought they were, then heard their voices again.

"Okay, okay, you're not fired. But you know what I did, man. I put my *house* on the line for this place. My goddamn house."

"I didn't let that kid in. Mike shoulda spotted him."

"They say they never spotted him."

"It was a packed house, man."

"Yeah, we pulled in the big bucks. . . . Sherry might have seen him. She says not, though. I coulda lost my house."

Travis listened, not moving, not calling attention to himself. He decided that all those years of writing, all that last year of working on the book, clobbering Stan, it was all a predictable chain of events leading up to this guy losing his house.

This is so totally weird, man, he thought. His face felt sticky. He hoped it was blood and not motor oil.

"And did you have to beat the kid up? Look at him. What if the cops come by?"

They were closer now.

"He had it comin'!"

"Okay." The owner was squatting down beside him. "Where do you live?"

"Cleveland," Travis muttered.

"Then forget me calling a cab."

"No." Travis rolled himself into a scrunched sitting position, huddling in his jacket. "Could you call my uncle?"

"Geez, Gary, you really whopped up on him."

"He had it comin'."

"I'm okay. Could you call my uncle?"

Travis was really tired of this scene. He dreaded the coming hangover.

When the owner left to call Ken, Gary kicked him again. "You had it comin'."

Travis didn't even feel it.

I sold my book. He clutched at the thought like a drowning man at a raft. He wanted to be somewhere quiet to think about it.

It wasn't on the ride home. He had never seen Ken this mad. The only thing saving him was Christopher sleeping in his car seat—Ken had to keep it down a little. Travis had forgotten Christopher was going to be at the ranch this weekend.

Ken pulled up at the back door. He paused for the first time since Travis had staggered into the car.

"Well."

"Well what?" Travis winced as he popped the door open.

"You have anything to say?"

"Yeah, I sure am glad I didn't have to listen to all that sober."

For a second Travis felt a stab of fear at the look on Ken's face. But somehow he came up with the bravado he'd faced the cops with.

"Chill out, man," he said. "It's my life."

He and Ken stared at each other in the white glare of the car's interior light. Travis waited, shivering, though he wasn't cold. . . .

"I used to say that," Ken said. There wasn't any irony in his voice at all, only a half-laughing wonder. "I remember saying that."

Later, watching the room spin, wishing he could throw up, Travis felt strangely comforted. It was really weird, but ever since Ken yelled at him, he hadn't seemed so lonesome anymore.

Chapter 6

His head felt like it was going to pulsate wide open, like a special effect in a horror movie. It was the price you had to pay for the party, he told himself, as he had many times before. You don't get something for nothing. But since the "something" seemed to be a swollen jaw, sore ribs, and a vague memory of talking to some girls, the price seemed a little steep.

Especially since Ken was still on his back. Travis sipped his orange juice and chewed his toast in silence, listening to Ken, thinking: Just as long as he doesn't kick me out. . . .

"I've got enough worries without chasing around after some drunk kid in the middle of the night."

"Look, man, I'm sorry they woke you up, I just couldn't think of who else to call."

"They didn't wake me up. I was already awake —wondering where the hell you were, what the hell you were doing, and asking myself why the hell had I let myself in for this."

"Why did you?" Travis asked. He'd started out with good intentions, but he was ready to chuck them. "And no more of this irony bullshit."

Ken looked slightly surprised that he knew the word *irony*. Then he sat down on the bar-stool across the island table. . . .

Finally he said, "The last time I saw Tim, we had a big fight. I guess you've figured out we didn't see eye to eye on the war. And the last thing I said to him was 'I hope you get blown right out of the sky, you fascist baby killer.'

"I wake up sometimes hearing those words. That's why you're here. And that's probably why you can still stay."

He picked up his coffee cup and left for the den.

Travis sat there. It was really weird, how he'd think he knew how he felt about things, then suddenly there'd be a sharp turn, and he'd end up in a place he wasn't expecting. Like his feelings were a bumper car, he'd have a grip on the steering wheel, and it still didn't go in the direction he'd thought it would.

It was raining. Casey wouldn't be giving lessons today. Maybe he'd go down to the barn later.

He poured himself another cup of coffee and went to the den.

Ken had Christopher on his lap, watching He-Man cartoons.

"Hey, I know what," Travis said. "You can ground me."

Ken smiled in spite of himself. Christopher wiggled off his lap to act out the cartoon, waving an imaginary sword at the villains.

"You know," Ken said, "one of the reasons I'm glad I waited so long to have a kid is, by the time he's a teenager, hopefully, I'll be too senile to care what he's doing. And, hopefully, I'll have forgotten what it's like to be one. Its been spooky enough, hearing myself say things to Chris that my parents said to me. Now I'm hearing things from you I remember saying. 'It's my life'—God, I remember that. And it doesn't seem so long ago either."

He absentmindedly switched channels. Bugs Bunny was blowing up Daffy Duck. Chris screamed in protest. "No more He-Man," Ken said. "Too violent."

The commercial seemed to appease Christopher immediately. "I want one of those," he said.

"In fact," Ken said to Travis, "I remember what it was like so vividly I feel like Achilles, in the *Iliad*, coming back from the land of the dead, like I've come back to tell you what it's like in the land of grown-ups."

"Not the *Iliad*," Travis said absently. The coffee was chewing a hole in his stomach. "The next one, where what's-his-name is trying to get home."

"My God," Ken said, slightly thunderstruck, "you're literate!"

"Yeah, yeah, I'm real literate." Travis finally remembered what it was that had caused this whole thing. "That's why I had to celebrate last night. I sold my book."

"What book?"

"I wrote this book and sent it to a publisher and it's going to get published. So I was trying to celebrate."

Ken looked skeptical. "Sorry, kid, I haven't gotten the impression you could write a compound sentence. You wrote a book?"

"Yeah, I write all the time. I'm really good at it too. Want to see the letter they sent me?"

He pulled the crushed envelope from his back pocket. A little mashed since he'd slept in his clothes, but still in one piece.

"You wrote a book all by yourself?" Ken scanned the letter quickly.

"Yeah, and I talked to Mrs.—Ms. Carmichael yesterday and she's coming here to talk about it."

"Why didn't you call me? I'd have joined you in a light beer or something. This is great!"

Finally there was someone to get excited with him. "I tried to, but you were in a meeting or something. And Mom wasn't home. Nobody was here. I just wanted to move for a while."

"You could have left a message—you haven't signed anything yet?"

Travis shook his head as he lit up a cigarette. "Don't sign anything until I read it."

"Okay. But I want to talk to the publisher by myself, when she gets here." Travis looked for an ashtray for his match and ended up stuffing it in his pocket.

"Sure. Sure. I can't believe this! I wonder if it's some kind of record, at your age? Call your mom."

Ken paused, then said, "You know, you could be dead from those things by the time you're fifty."

"Hopefully," Travis said, in a very good imitation, "I'll be too senile to care."

"Flirting with death," Ken said. "I remember doing that." But he didn't sound mad.

Travis remembered, on his way to the kitchen phone, that he'd meant to let Ken know he was sorry about last night—he was, too, because in a funny kind of way he cared about his uncle now, more than just as someone who was keeping him out of a juvenile home. Somehow, he thought he had, though nothing had been said.

He called Mom and listened impatiently to her dazed exclamations, and spent more time than he should have on a call to Joe, who mainly wanted to know how much money he would get, would he sell it to the movies, would Travis get to be in *People* magazine?

Although Travis had asked himself the same questions, he hung up peeved and restless. Nobody, absolutely nobody, seemed to grasp what this meant. It meant he really was a *writer*.

Well, hell, he thought, *he'd* known that since second grade.

He got cleaned up and went down to the barn—he was anxious to see Casey (he still half thought, maybe half hoped, he wasn't in love with her)—and he was anxious to get away from Christopher, who was nagging him to play trucks. Ten minutes of playing trucks was all Travis could stand.

He wasn't surprised to see that the Star Runner was still in his paddock, in spite of the rain—in his stall he kicked the walls until the rest of the horses were nervous wrecks. Casey kept putting him in the stall to eat, she said he had to be stalled at the shows so he had to get used to it, but it had to be pretty bad weather for her to bring him in for a long time.

God, he's big, Travis thought, hurrying by him. The Star Runner stood staring over the top of the gate. You didn't notice how big he was until you stood next to him, because of his proportions. Nothing gangly, or too heavy—a perfectly streamlined horse. Only big.

He finally noticed Travis, whirled, and flashed across the paddock, splattering mud.

"Thanks a lot," Travis muttered, brushing off his jacket, then wiping his hands on his jeans. He jogged into the barn and almost bumped into the white pony.

"Hey, Silver Hawk, what are you doin', wandering around loose?" He looked around, grabbed a halter off a stall door, and fastened it around the pony's head. Silver Hawk, who had the disposition of a cocker spaniel, stood docilely, snuffling Travis's pockets for carrots.

"Hey, Casey?" he yelled. One of the stall doors was open, the wheelbarrow parked outside. Travis knew by now that if you had to clean a stall with the horse still in it, you used the wheelbarrow to block the door. Something is really weird here, he thought. "Casey?"

Robyn stepped out of the stall. She wasn't wearing a shirt. She wasn't wearing a bra.

"Casey went to the feed store."

Travis said, "Oh."

He hadn't noticed the Jeep was gone. He remembered one time Kirk yanking him out of the street, saving him from a passing truck, laughing. "You'll walk into a burning building, someday. . . ."

He remembered that, listened to the rain, felt the pony's nose nudging him, and all the while he never took his eyes off Robyn.

"I got hot," she said. "I've been strip-searched for drugs four times. I've got to where I'm good at taking my clothes off."

Travis knew she was stoned. He'd never liked

Robyn, never understood why Casey had hired her.

Well, hell, he thought, looking around for a place to tie the pony, what's "like" got to do with it?

"Robyn"—Casey's voice behind him made him jump—"you're fired."

She didn't sound mad, but she did sound final.

"Okay." Robyn dropped her shovel, picked up her shirt, and walked out of the barn. Travis felt his face flaming. He hadn't even thought of Casey coming in.

Casey took the pony's lead rope and put him back in the stall.

"I should have done that a long time ago."

"Listen," said Travis, "I didn't have anything to do with that."

"Good. No tellin' what you would have caught."

"Why'd you ever hire her, anyway?"

"She used to be a really good rider," Casey said. "She was one of the best."

Travis had heard before that Robyn rode, but one of the best?

"We both started training with Jessie Quincy when we were twelve. Robyn was a natural. As good as I was, believe it or not. You want a job?"

"Me? Doin' what?"

"Stable hand, groom—I'm not proposing. And if I ask you to water the horses, you don't hose them down."

Travis saw she wasn't trying to bug him, and grinned wryly. "Yeah, I'd like a job."

"Think you can learn to tell a pelham from a snaffle?"

"Sure. Those different kinds of horses?"

Casey sighed. "Different kinds of bits."

"That's the part that goes in their mouth, right?"

Casey rolled her eyes.

"Look," Travis said, "I can learn that stuff. I used to work for a vet, I'm good with animals."

"Okay. There's the shovel, there's the stalls." Casey turned to go into the tack room.

"Hey, Casey."

She stopped.

"Whatever happened to her, Robyn?"

"Everything wonderful. She was winning like crazy, her dad was buying her thirty-thousand-dollar horses, flying her to Dallas every weekend to ride with a big trainer, putting her on the Arizona circuit, aiming her toward the Olympics . . ."

Travis waited for the tragedy. Maybe the dad died. Maybe a crippling fall. . . .

"The catch was, Robyn didn't want all that. She wanted to ride for fun, not ride for her dad's ego trip. It was like her riding wasn't *hers* anymore. You've got to have talent to do this, but you've got to have will too. It was like the only way out of it for her was to get fat and fried. Well, I had to get rid of her. It could have been one of the pony moms walking in just now."

Travis picked up the shovel, writing up Robyn's story in his head. He'd give the dad a mustache, and a silver Rolls. . . .

He opened the stall door, and wished, again, that he didn't have a hangover.

The barn was quiet, except for the rain drumming lightly on the roof. Casey never had the radio on when she was here alone. He could hear her on the phone with a pony parent. It amazed him how patient she was with the parents. Anxious parents, pushy parents, parents who seemed to think buying lessons meant buying the trainer —some were okay, and tried to be helpful, but once, after listening to a mother raving about a ribbonless show—was it the pony's fault, did she need a new pony? And, it was implied, a new trainer?—Travis said, "Why do you put up with that stuff?"

Casey replied, "It's my paycheck. I need to earn a living. It comes with the territory. If it was just training horses, it wouldn't be work."

Now he listened to her explaining why a class of five couldn't be rescheduled around one grandparent's visit and thought: Whatever they're paying her, it's not enough.

He'd also been listening to a dog barking outside, Ken's old Labrador by the sound of it, and it seemed to be getting more and more excited.

Travis decided to go take a look. Maybe Motorboat had caught a rabbit, which seemed to be one of his great goals in life lately.

It was the biggest snake he'd ever seen, coiled and lunging at the dog, who jumped and kept barking.

Biggest, hell. As far as he knew it was the only snake he'd ever seen, and he couldn't account for the revulsion and almost mindless terror that he felt.

And then he saw Motorboat, flattened into a stalking position, eyes glittering, creeping up by fractions of inches, getting ready to go in for the kill.

He had the shovel in his hands, swinging the edge at the snake, yelling at the dog to get back, knowing he was going to trip over the damn mutt and fall right on top of the snake. He got the head pinned as Motorboat leapt on the thrashing body, grasping with his teeth, thumping hard with his hind claws. The head was severed with a sickening crunch before Travis realized he was using all his strength on the shovel handle.

The headless body still twisted, Motorboat still fought it, and Travis ran back into the barn to get Casey. He slid to a stop, thinking: If the body was still moving, the head . . .

He turned back. The Lab was barking at Motorboat now, who seemed to be torn between batting the snake's body and clawing the dog.

The snake's head lay in the wet grass, and

Travis poked at it with the shovel, intending to scoop it up and put it in the trash barrel. Suddenly it seemed to disappear. Travis lifted the shovel, searching the ground. Then he saw that the severed head had bitten onto the edge of the shovel, and hung there, staring at him.

"Goddamn." He half sobbed, shuddering, sickened, amazed. He didn't throw the shovel, screaming, although the thought flashed across his mind. He carried the head to the trash burner and shook it off.

Casey was standing in the doorway.

"That was a water moccasin. They're poisonous, did you know that?"

"I knew it was a snake." Travis shrugged off the creeps. She was looking at him like he was a person, not a nephew, a hired hand.

"Pretty brave," she said.

The excitement of the fight was ebbing, leaving him chilled and nauseated. But he went back into the barn to finish the stalls.

Brave. It wasn't a word Casey used lightly.

He was on his way through the house to the shower when the phone rang. He picked it up on the third ring, not sure if Ken was home or not, and was surprised to hear Mom's voice. He'd just talked to her, and Stan was a real miser about long-distance calls.

"Honey," she said finally, after all the how-are-yous and how's-everyones, "Stan wants to read your book."

"I'll send him a copy." Travis grinned, picturing the way he'd autograph it.

"No, I mean, he wants to read it now, before it's published." Her voice faded and picked up. "He wants to make sure there's nothing in it about him."

For a moment Travis froze. Then he said quite calmly, "Well, he can't. I don't need his okay on my book. It's got nothing to do with him."

"Travis, hon, don't be upset, but you know you can't sign a contract until you're eighteen, I'll have to sign for you—"

"And you won't until Stan reads it, right?"

The phone hammered against his head and Travis had to grip it with both hands. "Well, he won't read it! I'll burn it first! I should have killed him when I had the chance!"

He could still hear Mom nattering away but couldn't make out a single word.

His fingers itched for the fire poker. "Goddamn it! Goddamn it!"

He yanked the phone off the wall and slammed it across the room.

It barely missed Teresa, who seemed to have materialized out of nowhere.

It barely missed Christopher.

Chapter 7

He couldn't stop pacing around in his room, because when he did he could feel his heart pounding so violently it scared him. He'd heard of kids his age having heart attacks. . . .

He didn't want to die now, not until he had one more crack at Stan—goddamn him! Motorboat had picked up on the vibes and was racing around the room too. Travis envied the way he could climb the curtains, jump up the walls, rip the stuffing out of the chair when he paused to sharpen his claws—Travis would have liked to be doing those same things.

Travis could hear, distantly, Teresa and Ken arguing. At one time he would have given anything to get an earful of a fight between those two to see what the deal really was: but now—

"You're not leaving him here with *him,* you're leaving him here with *me,"* Ken said.

Travis heard that one, along with Christopher's crying. The whole damn house was a storm center, just because of that beer-bellied jerk hundreds of miles from here. He'd get even. You bet he'd get even. If he had to hitchhike back, steal a gun, buy an axe—

After what could have been minutes, or hours, Travis came out. It had been quiet awhile, Teresa was gone. He wanted to tell Ken what Stan was pulling. Maybe there was something legal he could do about it. Boy, he bet Ken would be mad—

And Ken did listen to him with that preoccupied silence that was a sure sign of fury. He listened to Travis's railings against Stan, his outrage at Mom's betrayal, his threats. They were dealing with somebody dangerous, now, man. He had nothing to lose! He'd burn that book if he had to, burn it page by page before he asked Stan's approval. Ken would talk to Mom, right? Ken would help him—

"I'll help you pack and drive you to the airport, that's what's going to happen."

Travis had a sudden flash: Ken's anger didn't have much to do with Stan. He sat down and stared across the coffee table at his uncle.

"Do you think I'll let you stay here and mess up my chances with Christopher? Teresa's going to fight me for custody and she'll use the fact that

I'm obviously living with a dangerous delinquent. Except after today I'm not going to be. Get packed."

Travis felt sick. There was nowhere for him. Mom would choose Stan, Ken would choose Christopher, anytime he started feeling safe, someone would jerk the ground out from under him. To his own horror and surprise he burst into tears.

"I thought you liked me." He sobbed, knowing he sounded like a baby, a girl, a moron, and tried to straighten up, get it together, but he was just too goddamn tired.

He'd thought he had been pretty brave through all this mess, had half hoped someone was going to pin a medal on him; but the truth was, everyone was too busy elsewhere.

"Oh, geez," he heard Ken mutter.

Travis got to his feet and managed to say, "I'll get ready."

He didn't know where Ken had put his suitcase, so he just started piling stuff on his bed. He wondered if he could live at home for a little while, at least till he bashed Stan again, before he was sent to the reformatory. But maybe Stan would get him first this time.

He couldn't stop crying. All the crying he hadn't done before was stored up, waiting for a chance like this, he hadn't even known he was carrying it around. But he knew it now.

I sold my book.

That wasn't any comfort now. It'd never get published, not till years from now when he was eighteen. Or maybe—he could admit it now—there was a possibility he'd break down, let Stan read it, get his goddamn approval. . . . Travis thought of trying to go on living after a humiliation like that. His spirit broken, not special anymore, nothing of his own. . . .

I'll rot in jail first, he thought. I'll kill myself, and I won't burn it. It'll get published.

Then he thought of what it was going to be like, never seeing Casey again. And Ken. He really *had* thought Ken liked him. . . .

"Look." Ken had opened the door, or maybe Travis had forgotten to shut it. "At least tell me why you threw the phone at Christopher."

Travis wiped his face with his old Led Zeppelin T-shirt. It was too small for him now, anyway.

"I didn't. I didn't see them. I was just so mad . . . I wasn't aiming at Christopher."

"Teresa said they'd been standing there a few minutes, you were ranting and raving over the phone, then you threw it at them. You mean you didn't see them all that time?"

"No, I was talking to Mom."

Ken stood there quietly. Travis hated the sound of his own sniffles, and blew his nose into the shirt. "Why would I throw a phone at Christopher, anyway?" He gulped.

"Well, Teresa thinks you're on drugs."

"I'm not on drugs. I don't even *like* drugs."

Which was basically true, although the one time he'd tried cocaine, he'd liked it so much it scared him. He'd seen people get to where all they thought about was that stuff and how to get it. Picturing himself throwing everything away like that scared him enough to never do it again.

"And you swear you didn't see them?"

"I was talking."

"Some people might find it hard to believe you can't talk and see at the same time," Ken said.

Travis held his breath. Maybe . . . maybe . . .

"But I've been around you long enough to believe it. You just look so normal it's easier to believe you're drugged instead of eccentric."

Eccentric. Travis connected that word with little old ladies living with hundreds of uncaged birds, or some professor with his lunch money pinned to his suit. . . .

"I'll talk to Teresa. Maybe we can give it another try. You just don't know how dirty a fight can get when it's about your kid."

That's right, Travis thought bitterly, I wouldn't know.

But he said, "Thanks."

Ken said, "Listen, one more thing. You do like drinking."

"Well, yeah, but I can usually hold it pretty good. I can usually put everybody under the table."

"That's one of the earliest signs of alcoholism. I don't know if anyone's told you," Ken said slowly, "but you're genetically programmed to be an alcoholic. Our dad—your grandfather—died in a veterans' hospital of cirrhosis. And now you've joined a profession that seems to encourage it, if I remember my English lit courses. I'd watch it if I were you."

So. His grandfather had been an alcoholic, huh? Ken was right, all the big-name writers seemed to be boozers. . . .

"How about my dad?"

"No, Tim was—actually Tim was capable of knocking back a few, in the right mood, who knows what . . . You know that saying Live fast, die young, and have a good-looking corpse? Cirrhosis is not all that fast, and what you leave's not pretty."

Great. Just when you were onto a good story, it turns into a lecture.

"Achilles says: What sometimes sounds like a lecture, is sometimes just the truth."

Travis jumped with surprise.

"I'm telling you, kid, it doesn't seem like that long ago, I was there."

Ken paused. "I'll talk to Teresa," he repeated.

The tears still wouldn't quit coming, although he wasn't sobbing anymore. Travis wadded the shirt around for a clean spot. "Tell her I'll piss in a bottle for her anytime."

He hadn't meant to be funny, but Ken took it that way, and chuckled all the way down the hall.

Travis started sticking his stuff back in the drawers. He finally paused with his T-shirt, deciding between the trash can and the dirty-clothes hamper. He finally put it in with the dirty clothes. He'd hang on to it a little bit longer. He could still stay, and this time it didn't have anything to do with Tim.

It was the hangover, he decided later. And the damn snake. He'd stayed in the shower so long the hot water ran out, and felt a little better. He wouldn't have been such a big baby if he hadn't been so hung over and tired. He hurt, too, with his sore ribs, and a backache from shoveling, you had to consider that.

He lay flat on his back. Motorboat lay on his chest, his paws tucked under him, staring at Travis with half-shut eyes, rumbling with a loud purr. Cats had such weird eyes. . . .

Ken knocked on the door, then said, "Telephone."

Travis had heard the phone, but figured it was probably Teresa making sure Ken hadn't been murdered by the frenzied drug fiend.

"I don't want to talk," Travis yelled.

Ken opened the door. "What?"

"Tell her Stan's not reading the book. Tell her—"

"It's Ms. Carmichael, you dope."

"Oh." He scrambled up, dumping Motorboat to the floor.

"Travis?" He recognized the voice on the phone.

"Yeah."

"I'm going to be in Denver next week for a convention, and I'd like to stop by on the way back. I'm really on a tight schedule, this is a hectic time of year for us, but could you meet me at the airport for lunch next Sunday? I'll have a few hours between planes."

"Yeah, I think." He looked at Ken. "Could you drive me to the airport Sunday?"

Ken nodded and Travis said, "Yeah, I can make it."

"Splendid. My flight is American 203 from Denver, and it's scheduled to arrive at one o'clock, so perhaps it will. Can you meet me at the gate?"

"Yeah." Travis wrote the flight down on the memo pad.

"What will you be wearing?"

"What?"

"How will I know you?"

"Uh, black T-shirt, brown leather jacket."

"You must dress like your characters."

She had it backward, his characters dressed like he did, but he said, "Yeah."

"Well, I won't be wearing a red rose, but I will be wearing a bright red dress. Very Santa Fe western, you won't be able to miss me. And, Travis,

you might bring along a copy of your manuscript.''

Red Santa Fe dress but no rose, Travis thought
frantically. Maybe Ken would know what she was
talking about.

"I don't have one"—he'd just realized what
she'd said.

There was a pause. "Who does?"

"You do."

"We have the only copy?"

"Yeah."

"You sent the original through the mail without
making a copy?"

"Yeah."

"Oh." There was another pause. "Well, I'll
have the office make us a few copies. See you next
week. Bye, now."

"Yeah."

He hung up the phone, dazed. She was the first
person he'd ever heard use the word *splendid*. He
wondered what she was going to look like. He had
absolutely no idea what a publisher was supposed
to look like. His characters. She knew how his
characters dressed. . . . He was going to meet a
publisher!

"Kid," Ken said, "you have the most incredible
way with words, on the phone."

Travis realized now that his every other word
had been *yeah*.

His face burned. Then he shrugged.

"Well, she's not publishing my phone conversations." He tried to seem careless, but it was hard not to jump up and down and turn somersaults.

"Can't blame her for that," Ken said. "You hungry? Let's go get pizza."

"I'm starvin', man," Travis said.

Chapter 8

"I don't see why I can't meet her by myself. I wrote it by myself, I figured out where to send it by myself, I mailed it by myself—"

"I've told you—you can have lunch with her without us. I'm just going to shake her hand, let her know you're not rattling around the universe like a loose pea, and go."

"Aw, she knows I got an uncle." Travis was nervous, and as usual, nervous got him irritated. He wanted to turn around and yell, "Shut up!" at Christopher, who was playing with an airplane in his car seat, complete with airplane noises.

It was bad enough that Ken was going to deliver him to Ms. Carmichael like it was his first day of kindergarten; Christopher was going to be there too.

Ms. Carmichael, meet the nursery class, he thought bitterly.

As if he'd been reading Travis's mind, Ken said, "Have you been avoiding Christopher lately? I thought you guys got along okay."

Travis winced. He'd hoped Ken hadn't noticed. "Well, I don't want to get him mad at me, and sometimes I can't help it."

"He gets mad at me, too, and I manage to live through it."

"Yeah, but he could get me kicked out." Travis thought Ken might as well hear the truth. He'd felt bad, because Chris couldn't figure out what was going on, but that phone-throwing episode had put a serious scare into Travis.

Ken was quiet so long Travis thought the subject was closed.

"I'm not saying you can't get kicked out." His voice was startlingly loud all of a sudden. "But Christopher can't do it."

"You sure?"

"Positive."

"Great." Travis was relieved. "You know, I didn't know little kids were like real people before. Like the horses, they're like real animals."

Ken said dryly, "Live and learn." And Travis didn't know if he was talking to himself or not.

"What airline?" Ken asked.

"Western. No—the dress is western. American."

"I hope you've got the flight right."

Travis hoped so too. He'd been doing so many screwy things since Ms. Carmichael's call, he couldn't swear to it.

"Daddy, you don't have a beard," Christopher said.

"No, I don't," Ken answered absently.

"David has a beard."

"Who's David?"

"Mama's friend."

Travis glanced sideways at Ken, and saw his jaw twitch. Geez, he thought, half in sympathy, half irritated, if he still cares about her, why doesn't he patch it up? It always bugged him to see adults being stupid. And they always act like they know everything. . . .

"What's Santa Fe western?" he asked suddenly.

"It's this artsy-fartsy cowboy stuff—East Coast western."

That didn't help him much. Red. Well, at least he knew what red was.

"Travis doesn't have a beard," Christopher said.

He did recognize her right away. Fairly tall, forty at least, wearing a bright red cowboyish dress, dark blue boots, carrying a dark blue brief-case-looking bag. Ms. Carmichael had long, wild, wiry black hair, pulled back at one side with a piece of turquoise, and large black eyes. She was the most glamorous person Travis had ever seen. This was style!

As she looked around the crowd he stepped out and waved at her.

"Travis?" She put out her hand, and after a second he shook it.

"Yeah," he said, then he could have bitten his tongue off. *That* word again.

"Nell Carmichael."

"This is my uncle," Travis added.

"Ken Harris." Ken shook her hand too. "And this is Christopher."

Christopher said, "I have to pee."

"Oh, dear," said Ms. Carmichael. "I do too. Let's go find a john."

Travis wished he could die, quickly and painlessly, right then and there, but Ken laughed and they walked down the hall together.

In the john he combed his hair carefully, for the hundredth time that day. Maybe he should have worn his olive-green long-john shirt. Maybe black was too . . . old? Tough?

"Do I look okay?" he asked Ken, who was trying to hold the water on, and trying to hold Christopher up to wash his hands, at the same time.

"You look fine."

Travis was dying to know what Ken thought of Ms. Carmichael, but they trooped back out to wait for her in silence.

Ken and Christopher left them at the restaurant entrance, much to the relief of Travis, who was expecting Chris to announce he wanted to do poo, too.

But after they were gone, he felt tongue-tied. He didn't know any small talk, and was scared he'd have to do some before they got to talking about the book.

"Your uncle is a very attractive man."

Travis shrugged. Ken probably did look good for as old as he was, but he didn't have any clothes style. Suits to work, jeans on weekends. Today he'd put on his corduroy blazer, and he was nothing to be ashamed of.

Travis looked at the menu, relieved to see hamburgers, wishing he could order a bourbon instead of a Coke. He'd probably end up knocking the damn Coke over. . . .

"And Christopher is a darling. Do you visit them often?"

"Naw, this is the first time." He didn't know how to explain *that*, so he shut up again. The waiter came and took their order.

"So," he said. "You gonna buy the book?"

Ms. Carmichael looked slightly startled at his directness, and he squirmed a little. There was probably some complicated bunch of rules to business lunches, and he didn't know them. But he'd stick with what he *did* know, and he wasn't going to sit here and chat about Ken, Chris, and the nice weather we're having.

After a moment she said, "Travis, who do you think would like to read your book?"

"Teenagers. Kids like me." He was sure they would because *he'd* read it and loved it.

"I agree. We have an extensive young-adult line, books we market directly to young people."

"Yeah, I know." Travis paused while the waiter set his hamburger in front of him. "That's why I sent it to you guys."

"Oh, so you're aware of marketing?"

Travis wasn't sure what that meant, so he didn't say anything. He'd just thought if you had a book about teenagers, you'd try a publisher who did books about teenagers. They sat in silence a minute while she poked at her salad and he put ketchup on his burger.

"Do you hang out in bookstores a lot? Do your friends?"

"Well, I do, but most of my friends don't."

"How do they get introduced to books?"

"I don't know—school, I guess. We have to do book reports. The library. Sometimes if we see a movie and there's a book . . . You ever see *Rambo*?"

"Travis, you mentioned schools. Schools are a very large part of the young-adult market. Teachers and librarians are some of our best salespeople. I think word of mouth will be fantastic on your book, but we'll have to get it to the kids initially."

Travis could barely sit still, he was getting so excited. She was talking about *his* book, like it really was a book, a book out there, *selling*!

"Yeah," he said.

"Well, frankly, no teacher or librarian wants to

lose his job. And recommending your book, as it is now, could cost someone his job."

It dawned on Travis what she was getting around to: "You want me to clean up the language? Hell, I'll clean up the language. No sweat."

"You don't have a problem with that?"

She was so relieved, Travis realized she didn't know he would have promised anything to get her to publish it. Almost.

"Naw, I can fix it. Everybody's going to know what they're saying, anyway."

"That point aside, we still have a few problems —no major girl characters, for instance, and the majority of book buyers your age are girls."

Travis's eyebrows met over his nose. "I'll clean up the language some, but I ain't going to turn it into a romance. Let the guys read it—there's nothing for guys to read anyway, if you're not into sci-fi."

She might as well get clear on this now. "I don't know what girls do, so I don't write about them. And that junk they like to read makes me barf."

"What do you like to read?"

"Some nonfiction, like biographies. Stephen King. Hemingway. I think I'm going to like Fitzgerald sometime, but not now."

"Not now?"

"Well, I tried to read one of his books once, the one where everybody is hanging out on the beach sippin' sherry, but I didn't get it. I figured if I read it now I wouldn't like it, so I'll give it another try when I get older."

"What makes you think you'll like it at all?"

Travis stopped, trying to define it. "I like the way his sentences feel," he said finally. "Smooth and cool like Laddie pencils."

"Are you a mystery fan?"

"No," Travis said flatly. "I hate it when the only reason to read something is to know what happens next."

"But that *is* a good reason to read something."

"Yeah. But it shouldn't be the only one."

It was amazing, to be talking about reading. He never talked about reading with anyone. And it was such a major part of his life. Sometime, he thought, someday, he'd get Ms. Carmichael to split a bottle of bourbon with him and they'd sit up all night and talk about books. . . .

She was talking about *his* book right now, and he focused back on the conversation.

". . . more style than you know what to do with. It's so full of energy, so sincere, you'll be able to get away with the melodramatics. But not twice, Travis. The critics won't be indulgent twice. You'll have to use some discipline on the next one."

Critics. Markets. Styles. This was really book talk! He tried to stay intent on her every word, but his mind was racing so fast it was hard to hear.

Grammar. His grammar could really stand some improvement, although stylistically it was right for the dialogue. His spelling was, well, imaginative. But the narrative flowed, there was a strong sense of place, and his characters—well, his characters were wonderfully realized human beings, everyone would come away from this book convinced that these people really existed. He'd have to cut some description, he really didn't have to describe everyone again in each chapter—

"Are any of these characters based on real people?"

"No," Travis said slowly. "Not exactly . . . but like, they're real to me. You know Dusty?"

"The one that gets killed in the car crash."

"Yeah. Well, he's made up, totally, but sometimes I think about him, sometimes he even shows up in my dreams, like a real person. It's weird. I just forget he's not real."

"Shouldn't there be at least one sympathetic adult, though? Surely you know *some* sympathetic adults. . . ." She paused. "Or any adults, for that matter."

"Yeah." He shrugged. "But this is about kids. What have adults got to do with it?"

Finally, the waiter brought the check. Travis felt a little funny about letting her buy lunch, but Ken, who knew about business lunches, said she should. To cover his awkwardness he spoke up. "So. You can fix up the spelling, huh?"

She smiled up at him and slipped her credit card back into her billfold. "You know, when we first met, I couldn't believe you had written that book. Your speaking style is so different from the way you write."

"I got two languages." He realized he meant "vocabularies." "One in my head and one in my mouth."

"Interesting. Save it for interviews. Think you'll be able to do interviews?"

"Oh, yeah. I'll figure it out."

"You should photograph beautifully—"

"Ms. Carmichael?"

"Yes."

"Will my mom have to sign the contract, since I'm not eighteen?"

"Yes. Is that a problem?"

"No. No problem."

They paused in the airport hallway to shake hands again; she was going to her next flight, he was going to meet Ken at the baggage claim.

"Are you working on anything now?"

Travis shook his head.

"Start something new, right now, get it going before this one comes out. First-novel block is a very real phenomenon. You know," she said carefully, "this is going to change your life."

Travis shrugged. "It was changing anyway."

Chapter 9

Casey was getting ready for the last big show of the season. She was out on the Star Runner when Travis caught the bus in the morning for school, and usually rode him again following the afternoon lessons. Travis worried about her, at school. If something happened, out there alone during the day, it'd be hours before anyone found her.

Once, on the weekend, when Ken had drifted down to watch, they nearly witnessed a major crash when the Star Runner threw a bucking fit in the corner and Casey put him over a four-foot fence anyway; she'd lost both her stirrups and nearly went over his head as he landed.

"I don't see why she does damn stupid stuff like that," he'd said. Ken answered, "It's her life, isn't it?" Travis wanted to slug him. But when Casey rode up laughing, they laughed too.

If only the Star Runner were just, just, well, normal. A normal horse. Jennifer's horse, Sandman, was high-strung, apt to spook at things and occasionally run out at a jump; Travis learned to watch it when he haltered him because he would bite.

But that was normal. Travis had always liked animals, had no trouble liking most of the horses. He'd been embarrassed once while brushing a pony, to realize he was listening for a purr. The signals the horses used weren't as blatant as cats' or dogs', but they were there.

The Star Runner . . . Travis and Jennifer were watching him trot up and down in the paddock, and Jennifer shivered.

"He's so creepy," she said. "You ever noticed his eyes? There's white showing all the way around. That's supposed to mean he's crazy."

"I can believe it." Travis had an idea for a story —an outer-space alien stuck on earth, but nobody'd know it since it looked like a horse.

"I don't see why Casey loves him so much."

"Love?" Travis couldn't believe she still didn't know better. "Let's ask her. Hey, Case."

Casey had just turned out the ponies in the next paddock. Now she joined them, hanging over the railing.

"Jennifer," Travis said, in a breathless Jennifer-voice, "doesn't know why you love the Star Runner so much."

He really liked Jennifer, but sometimes she was so sweet it irritated him.

"Love?" Casey unknowingly echoed Travis. "Hell, the day he stops jumping I'll shoot him."

"Oh, Casey!" Jennifer was horrified.

"She'd do it," Travis agreed. Then, because he was sorry he'd mocked her, he started tickling her, and ended up chasing her back to the barn.

When he looked back, Casey was still watching the Star Runner. Waiting.

The Thursday night before the show, Travis worked late in the barn. He had to pack tack, make sure the big eight-horse trailer was clean, leg-wrap some of the horses. He'd learned how to pull manes, so that they were short and easy to braid, but the braiding itself, weaving a small strand and knotting it, was beyond him. Christopher could have done a better job.

Kelsey stayed for an extra hour and got four horses braided. They looked classy with the little row of knots down their necks. Travis assumed braiding was just to make them look better, but Kelsey said braiding had been started to keep manes from getting tangled in brush on the hunt field.

Casey was working on post entries. Some people had made up their minds about what classes to enter, or to go at all, at the last second. He remembered a dream he had the night before, involving Casey and her long legs. . . .

"Through?" Her voice made him jump.

"Just about." He turned away, afraid she'd see him reddening.

"Put the light blanket on Silver Hawk, would you? He's fairly clean right now, but those white ponies can get filthy overnight."

"Okay." Travis paused to study her handwriting. She printed, in strong clean lines, like a child.

When he went back to the house and saw Teresa's car but not Ken's, he almost turned around and went back. Being alone with Teresa was not something he looked forward to.

Well, hell, he thought, at least this time he knew she was in the house. Maybe if he made a good impression on her, she wouldn't give Ken such a hard time about splitting custody. He slammed the door so he wouldn't be surprising her.

"Ken?"

Travis went on into the living room. "Naw, it's me."

Teresa glanced up from the photo album she'd been looking through and took another sip of red wine.

"Oh. Hi. I brought Chris early, I've got to leave town again, tomorrow. It looks like Ken's going to be late."

Travis thought: Leaving with David? but didn't say anything. It obviously wasn't her first glass of wine.

"Been working in the barn?"

"Yeah." Travis hoped she could tell by the way he was dressed, not by the way he smelled.

"Ken said you'd been helping Casey. I wish that girl would wear some sun block."

Travis couldn't make that connection, but said, "Yeah. Hey," he added, "I'm sorry about the other night. I didn't mean to scare you guys."

Teresa nodded. She had beautiful dark deer-eyes, like Christopher's.

"Ken told me you were having a fight with your mom. She called earlier, by the way. She sounds real sweet. You ought to talk to her."

"She doesn't care about me," Travis said, the anger at her betrayal flooding back. "She doesn't even *know* me. She had a baby once, and still loves it."

"Well, honey, don't knock it. That's the strongest hold you'll ever have on anybody."

She went back to her pictures, but something made Travis think: She's picturing the fights she'll have with Chris when he's my age.

Ken had already made him feel peculiar that way; sometimes he'd look from Chris to Travis with an expression just short of horror. Like: *This is what's coming.*

"You ever see these?" Teresa held out the album. "Ken and I took a trip to Morocco in—oh, a long time ago. We took a freighter over, slept in train stations, on decks, in fifty-cent rooms."

"Geez, did you guys really look like that?" Travis stared at the photos. Teresa was so young-looking, really skinny, her hair longer and darker, parted in the middle and hanging down her back. She was wearing granny glasses and an Indian headband. She said that was Ken with her, but he wasn't even recognizable, with his hair to his shoulders and a drooping walrus mustache around his mouth. Both had on outlandishly long bell-bottomed jeans and gauzy Eastern shirts.

Travis was flabbergasted. Sure, he'd heard about hippies and stuff, but to actually have walked around looking like that! Didn't people laugh?

"This was my Gloria Steinem look. I think Ken was supposed to be Elliot Gould."

This didn't help Travis much, since he didn't know who those people were.

"I'm really glad we did that once, scrounging around and sleeping on sidewalks—but Ken's really sad we won't do it again."

"Yeah." Travis was on an entirely new train of thought. "So—you guys were into drugs and everything?"

"You think you invented it?" Teresa laughed, then said quickly, "You ought to know by now Ken is no substance abuser. Oh, no. Ken has entirely too much control for that." Teresa polished off her wine and said, "Would you get me just another half glass?"

When he brought it he said, "How'd you guys mess up, anyway?"

"What's Ken's story?"

"Well, when I asked him all he said was 'It all started with the Cuisinart.' "

"Sounds like him." She went on turning the pages of her album, and Travis gave up on getting a straight answer. Adults probably didn't even know straight answers anymore.

"You ever see Ken at the barn?" she said suddenly.

Travis thought it over. "Not much," he answered. Ken never did go to the barn, other than to stop by with a message or watch for a second. Travis had never seen him on a horse.

"See? It was always his big dream to raise quarter horses, and when that didn't work out just the way he planned, he quit the whole thing. He just can't stand any deviation from the plan.

"I just don't think I'm working out the way he planned either."

"So—Ken got into being a lawyer to help people and all that stuff?"

"Don't be silly. Ken got into being a lawyer because he thought he could make money. Don't get him wrong. Ken likes having money, it's just spending it that bothers him . . . well, he grew up poor and I didn't, what do I know? And—don't tell him I said this—but the law's just up his alley. He always did want to know the rules, the penalties . . . I just think there's more than one dream to have. And I don't know why happiness shouldn't be as trustworthy as any other emotion."

Travis was ticked off now. Garbage. She was sad, Ken was sad, why didn't they do something?

Ticked off, and scared too. Not me. Not me. I'll always know what I want, how to get it. . . .

She said, "You ever have to read that poem at school, about the guy sitting in the snow at the fork in the road, wondering about the road not taken?"

"Yeah." Travis had read it, but not at school. He just liked Robert Frost.

"What they don't tell you is, every time you turn around there's another goddamn fork."

He didn't think he'd be able to sleep that night, but he conked out immediately. He was real surprised to find Teresa in the kitchen the next morning, making pancakes with Christopher.

"Hi," she said cheerfully as he poured himself some coffee. She didn't look at him. He managed "Hi" with a straight face, but it was real hard to keep from smirking when he ran into Ken at the bottom of the stairs.

"Teresa thought she'd stay over," Ken explained, a little too rapidly. "She doesn't like to drive when she's been drinking."

"Yeah," Travis said. "Sure."

When their eyes met, Ken grinned and turned red.

Travis was oddly happy the rest of the day, though he couldn't put his finger on just why.

Chapter 10

Girls and horses! What was the big deal about girls and horses? It was weird. It was almost sick. At first he thought being at the show, being surrounded by cute girls in skintight breeches, was going to drive him horny-crazy; he could understand now what had happened to the twins—why if you worked at McDonald's, the sight of a fry could make you sick.

They petted the horses, fussed over them, combed and brushed them like they were going to a prom. Baby-talked them and even kissed them! That was a definite turnoff. He didn't get it. Like, he loved Motorboat, but couldn't imagine ever carrying on like this.

He was grumpy anyway. Five o'clock in the morning wasn't his favorite time to get up. It wasn't a bad time to go to bed sometimes, it usually meant a pretty good night before; but there wasn't anything great about a five o'clock rising.

And here it was eight-thirty, the show had been going on for a half an hour, and he'd been too busy to go watch anyone.

He was helping a frantic Jennifer tack up for her first class. Somehow it didn't surprise him that she was late.

He barely had the throatlatch of Sandman's bridle buckled when Jennifer grabbed the reins and trotted him out.

"Tell Casey I'm in the schooling ring."

"Where is she?" Travis hadn't seen her for an hour.

"Small arena." Jennifer's voice floated back. "With the ponies."

Casey was standing by the rail next to a woman Travis recognized as one of the pony moms, although he wasn't sure which.

Molly was leading Silver Hawk out of the arena, picking up a yellow ribbon on her way out.

"You really got a good deal on that pony," Casey was saying. "He's going great for her."

"Yes," said the mom. "But, well, I wish we'd found a chestnut."

Casey looked blank. "A chestnut?"

"You know Sarah Jerome has that little palomino that just matches her hair. They look so cute together."

"Matches her hair," Casey repeated calmly.

Travis felt he had to do something quick, so he said, "I know, you can dye Molly's hair white."

While the mom gave him a you-smart-ass look, he pulled Casey along with him.

"Jennifer's in the schooling ring, come on, she's late."

They were across the road when Casey spoke again. "I won't have to dye my hair to match my horse. Another year in this business will turn it solid gray. Match her hair! My God!"

And suddenly she gave him a slap on the back and said, "Good for you, kid."

The schooling ring was chaos. There were two jumps set up in the middle of the ring, side by side. Trainers stood by the jumps, yelling instructions, praise, abuse, while the riders came from both directions, sometimes narrowly missing head-on collisions. There were frantic yelps of "Heads up!" which Travis took to mean "Watch out!" And all around the ring people were warming up, trotting or cantering, the horses bucking and kicking if a stranger got too close behind. Travis thought the whole mess looked like some bizarre sort of horse bumper-cars.

"Leg-in-front-of-the-jump."

Travis recognized the voice and realized Casey had dodged through the traffic to stand by a jump, and Jennifer and Sandman were taking it.

"Again," Casey shouted. "And don't jump out in front of him."

Sandman cleared the poles easily and beautifully, barely missing a little girl on a black pony.

Travis heard the announcer on the loudspeaker. "Beautiful Day on deck. One away, Forget Me Not. Two away, Sandman. Three away . . ."

"You know your course?" Casey shouted, and Jennifer shook her head. Travis handed her the number as they left the schooling ring to stand with the others just outside the gate of the big indoor arena.

"Oh, bless you," Jennifer breathed, tying the strings around her waist so the number 263 was clear across her back.

A girl on a dark bay was in the arena.

"That first line should be an easy five, let him start rolling in the warm-up circle. The second inside diagonal is the tricky part—use all your ring, deep in the corner—see there, see there—"

The bay slid to stop and his rider nearly went over his neck onto the jump—"She cut in too quick, didn't give him enough distance. Be sure and go deep in the corner. And, Jenna, don't get antsy on that last single. Just stay the same, you don't have to be making any moves. It'll seem like you're not seeing the spot, but just wait for it. It'll be there. Now, what's your course?"

"Outside, diagonal, outside, diagonal, single."

"Okay, try to let him move on out right away—but the first line can be a short six if it has to, just make it smooth."

Travis said, "A short six what?"

"Strides. Twelve feet. A normal horse stride is twelve feet. You allow six feet on either side of the jump. The course is set for a certain number of strides between jumps. If you goof up, too fast, too slow, take the jump too big or too close, you have to decide to lengthen or shorten to the next jump." Casey used her teaching voice.

"Oh," Travis said. And he had thought the big deal was to stay on. He didn't see how Jennifer learned the course from watching one person go —he wasn't sure which jump she was supposed to take first, much less the order of the rest of them. The girl on the bay pulled him up into a finishing circle and left by a gate at the other end of the arena. Casey opened the entry gate and Jennifer trotted in.

"On course, two sixty-three Sandman, ridden by Jennifer Hailey."

Jennifer circled, picking up a canter, and Casey leaned on the rail, muttering to herself—once, as Jennifer went by, she said, "Clear into the corner," and as she came at the last fence, "Steady, steady," but to Travis it looked as though she'd had a perfect round—at least Sandman cleared all the jumps and hadn't stopped anywhere.

Casey ran outside to be there as Jennifer came out.

"Not bad, not bad, late with that second lead change and he chipped in a little at the gate, but you've got a shot at pinning."

Jennifer nodded, too breathless to speak. She smiled at Travis, her lipstick unnaturally bright in her white face.

"I always forget to breathe, on course. Casey, wait—listen, what time do you think it'll be over tonight?"

Casey paused. "Look, you know I can't time these things."

"I'm sorry," Jennifer apologized. "I just have piano recital tonight."

"You're in the last class and it's your shot at a medal, so you decide." Casey disappeared into the schooling ring again.

Jennifer slid off. "She's trying to quit smoking," she said. "It's making her mean. Well, we had a good first round, anyway, didn't we baby?" She patted Sandman's neck. "Such a good boy. *Such* a good boy."

Travis winced. It was a wonder the horses didn't puke.

"That was real pretty, honey." An older woman in jeans and a western jacket paused beside Jennifer. "You looked real nice."

Jennifer shivered. "Oh, thanks, Mrs. Kencaide. I'm just glad it's over. I'm not like Casey, I'm scared to death before every class."

The woman said simply, "Then why, child, do you do it?"

Jennifer opened her mouth, then shut it. You could tell she couldn't come up with a real good reason and hadn't tried to before.

"You must be Katherine's new groom."

Travis was still uneasy with the word *groom*. It made him feel like he should be standing on top of a wedding cake.

"Uh, I'm workin' for Casey Kencaide."

"That's right. K.C.—Katherine Caroline. I'm her momma."

Oh. So that was where she'd gotten her name. Hastily Travis said, "Nice to meet you," and shook her hand. He'd be nice to her and get her to talking—he'd learned from Ken and Teresa it was easy to get somebody talking about their kid. So now he knew her real name—who knew what he could pick up next?

"I'll see you around," he called, as Amber ran up, wanting help with her bridle.

The show went real slow. It seemed to Travis that there were hours of nothing to do—messing around at the stalls, hanging out in the stands watching the rounds (he was bored after ten minutes); able to tell if someone fell off, or if the horse stopped at a jump, but other than that having no idea what the judges' were judging by.

Casey was either running from one arena to the other—the ponies and low jumps were showing in the smaller barn, the more advanced riders and horses in the larger arena—or shouting instructions in the schooling ring, or hanging out with the other trainers, comparing horses and riders.

Travis watched Kelsey slink out of the ring after the off-course whistle blew, her hands held over

her face, squealing, "Ohmigod, I'm *so* embarrassed"; Amber's black pony refused three times
and she was dismissed from the ring; the older
lady, Mary, had a perfectly smooth round, which
would net her a third, and Travis heard Casey
remark, "The kids are more supple, the kids are
braver, but the older riders can *think*."

He overheard something else. He ducked into
the curtained-off tack stall to look for Amber's
spurs. Casey was in the stall right behind him,
hidden by the curtains, brushing the bay gelding
she was riding in the pregreen classes, and he
heard someone say, "God, Casey, where'd you
get that foxy groom?"

"He's Ken Harris's nephew. At first I wondered
how a classy guy like Ken could have such a sleazy
punk relative, but he's really okay. He's good with
the horses."

"Well, watch out for him. I think some of the
girls are planning to kidnap him. Is that your
pregreen?"

Travis didn't stay any longer. He ducked into
the men's room and stared, puzzled, into the
cracked and dirty mirror.

Sleazy punk. She must be crazy. His hair was
way too long to look punk. Damn hicks around
here probably had never even *seen* a punk! And
sleazy?

Suddenly he thought of something else: Ken
saying, "Sorry, kid, you haven't given me the impression you could write a complex sentence."

And Ms. Carmichael saying, "I don't believe you wrote this book." And just last week his English teacher had kept him after class to say, "You know, your attitude problem is really starting to bug me. And I thought you might like to know that behavior is counted in my grading."

He had been shocked and outraged. What attitude?

"So what am I doing?" He certainly wasn't talking in class—he wasn't talking much in school.

"Oh, you know, slouching back there with that sneer on your face—if you get your grade knocked down much lower you'll flunk."

"Big flunkin' deal," Travis had said, and she'd sent him to the principal. She must have had PMS.

Now, though, he wondered about this weird impression people were getting of him. Sleazy punk. Was that what everybody thought?

He stared miserably at the mirror and a wave of homesickness almost knocked him down. He'd been so cool at home. . . .

He made sure he sat next to Casey's mom during the pregreen class.

"You ever get nervous about Casey jumping?" he asked her. Earlier one of the pony-kids' moms had gotten hysterical when the kid fell off and had the wind knocked out of her.

"Hell, no, honey. Life's way too short to get nervous about."

Mrs. Kencaide looked older than she was, brown and weather-beaten, her short brown hair teased up like a lot of ladies her age—like at one point in their lives they'd learned The Hairstyle and never ever thought about getting another. Travis's mom wore her hair almost the same.

She lit up a cigarette and Travis was suddenly horrified to realize all those little lines around her mouth came from inhaling. . . .

For the first time in three years he thought about quitting smoking.

"No, I was a barrel racer myself, and I always thought Katherine would want to rodeo—then my brother took us to the big Charity Horse Show one year, I reckon Katherine was eleven, and we saw the jumping. She says, 'Momma, I *got* to do that,' and I says, 'Okay, honey, let's figure you out a way'—'cause I knew Katherine, and her mind was made up."

She paused. Travis had had a hard time understanding her drawl—she sounded so country-western, and that was one kind of music he couldn't stand.

"So, what'd you do, get her lessons?"

"Sorry, honey, I was just watchin' that round. Those ol' quarter horses are the kind I like. That one is quicker than a cat, ain't he? Some of these skinny ol' Thoroughbreds look like poor feeders to me. Oh, yeah, well, I couldn't afford any fancy lessons, but my brother, he's a horse trader and an auctioneer and he asked around about jumpin' trainers, and he heard this lady, Jessie Quincy, was supposed to be the best. And I drove Katherine over there and she talks Ms. Quincy into lettin' her work in exchange for lessons; Ms. Quincy done that with a couple of other little gals and sometimes it worked out, and sometimes it didn't; but she never had anybody who worked like Casey, both groomin' and ridin'. Time she's sixteen she was gettin' paid to ride, she was giving lessons.

"About a year ago she turned pro, and at the same time my brother tells us Ken Harris is lookin' to lease his barn. There was a crazy bronc out at the Circle J racing stables that keeps jumpin' out of his paddocks. Real fast, my brother says, but so loco none of the jockeys want to mess with him. The owner was ready just to put him down.

"Casey came back from lookin' at him and she says, 'Momma, this is it.'"

"Is what?" Travis asked.

He saw that Mrs. Kencaide was watching the entry gate where Casey had ridden up on the bay.

It took him a couple of seconds to recognize her; she'd been wearing a sweat suit over her riding breeches and white shirt to keep them clean. She was in a dark gray riding jacket and black velvet hard-hat; her long legs in knee-high black boots. She looked like an elegant Park Avenue preppy. It was the first time he'd seen her wearing lipstick.

"On course, Casey Kencaide on Secret Sam."

All the horses had barn names, what everyone

called them at home, and show names, that they went by at shows. Travis thought it was kind of goofy. Secret Sam was called Stinker at home.

Casey made a large warm-up circle, trotting the bay around several of the jumps. A lazy, almost deadhead horse on the flat, Stinker got nervous jumping, and Travis realized Casey was letting him get a look at the jumps. She put him into an easy canter for the first line, got him back under control as he tried to run away after the second— he spooked out at the red brick wall, but Casey made him come back and drove him over it to finish the course.

There was a smattering of applause from the stands, but as Casey left the ring she looked back to the stands to her mother and smiled.

"That's my gal," Mrs. Kencaide said. "I knew I had me a lion cub right from the start."

Travis had a sudden bite of envy, mixed with homesickness, mixed with missing his own mom and being disgusted with himself for it. He left the stands hastily.

So why does *she* have to be the only kid I know who *likes* a parent? he thought sourly as he took Stinker's reins.

"Cool him off a little before you untack him," Casey said.

She was the first person he'd seen coming out of the arena breathing normally.

"I'd have whacked him one for running out like that," he said.

"He hasn't jumped enough to know if he likes it. I want him to like it. I hope Amber's in the schooling ring."

Casey ran off and Travis ran the stirrups up the stirrup straps so they wouldn't flap around.

"I'll cool him off for you." It was Kelsey.

"No, it's my job," Travis snapped at her. He was vaguely aware that Kelsey had a crush on him, just as he realized the mild commotion he was causing at the show. Males were few and far between in this sport. But he was so sick of girls. Just one night, just one night of cruising with his old buddies and tossing down a few beers and talking, *really* talking . . .

Something grabbed him around the leg. The first thing that flashed across his mind was a sex-crazed dog—it was Christopher.

"Hey," he said, "don't scare the horse."

"You wouldn't say hi." Christopher looked up at him with Teresa's dark eyes. "We said hi."

"Geez, kid, you do live in outer space half the time, don't you?"

Travis realized that Ken was standing right in front of him, trying to get his attention.

"What's up?" he said finally.

"We've been to get haircuts."

It shows, Travis thought. A haircut shouldn't look, well, new like that. For a panicked second he wondered where he'd go around here—surely there was a SuperCuts somewhere. . . .

"And your mom called. She's been trying to tell

you she'll sign the contracts after all. She wants you to call her later."

"Oh." So he'd won! Beat ol' Stan out on this one! "Great."

"Whooee." Another guy about Ken's age came up to them, holding a little girl by the hand. He was staring around at the riders. "This is paradise."

Dirty old geezer, Travis thought.

"This is my friend Steve Slade," Ken said. "My nephew, Travis."

"The famous writer?" Steve said, shaking his hand. Travis looked at Ken, who shrugged.

"So I bragged a little."

Travis felt like laughing out loud. Everything suddenly looked brighter. "What's up?"

"We bachelor dads are going to go eat pizza and watch football and let the kids kill each other."

Travis had a second of longing to go with them. . . . Geez, just to be around some *guys*—

"Daddy," the little girl said suddenly, "I want a pony."

"Sure, honey," Steve said. "We'll see."

"I *must* have a pony," she insisted. Ken and Steve laughed.

Travis watched her watching the ponies, and knew Steve had nothing to laugh about.

"So, you gonna sign the contracts?"

He didn't mean to sound so sharp—the day at

the horse show had just about done him in. He'd missed Casey's hunter round on the Star Runner (there seemed to be some big difference between "hunter" and "jumper" classes, but he hadn't figured out what) because he was rushing around helping Amber tack up—and it turned out to be the wrong class anyway.

And the Star Runner had slammed on the brakes at a four-foot wall and Casey went over his head to land on it. Travis was convinced she had broken some ribs, but she refused to go to the emergency room and had actually laughed when he suggested not riding tomorrow.

So even though he was glad to talk to Mom, and excited about the contracts, it was hard to get his mind off the show. It was like his mind had turned into a seesaw, sometimes the book was the high part and everything else disappeared, sometimes it was Casey and these goddamn horses, and sometimes it raced up and down till he was dizzy.

"Yes, I am, hon. You were right, the book is something you did on your own—"

"How's Stan takin' this?" he asked suddenly. "He's not beatin' up on you?"

"Oh, no, hon, Stan's never beat up on me. Travis, where'd you get such an idea?"

Are you nuts? he wanted to shout, but instead said, "Must be my vivid writer's imagination."

"Honey, you know except for those two times when he was unemployed and I was naggin' him, Stan's never hit me."

Travis didn't say anything and she added, "And if you'd been halfway nice to him you wouldn't have gotten hit either."

She sounded like she was crying. Travis rolled his eyes. This'd teach him to call home.

"Hey"—he changed the subject—"how's Joe doin'?"

"I don't know, he hasn't been around lately." She sniffled. "How's the cat?"

The cat. Travis suddenly realized Motorboat hadn't been around much lately either.

"He's in the barn a lot, there's mice out there."

Motorboat, in fact, had become obsessed with the mice, and Travis couldn't get his attention. And the cat had sort of fallen in love with Silver Hawk, leaping from the gate to his back, where he huddled and did happy paws, purring like an electric drill. He sat in the pony's food box while it ate, and rolled in the dirt in front of the jumps when Molly rode, apparently never dreaming he could be trampled.

And now Travis realized he'd been so preoccupied himself he hadn't really cared.

"Well, I'm glad he's earning his keep."

"Hey," Travis said hotly, "I'm workin' now, I'm giving Ken some board money."

"Honey, I didn't mean . . ."

Suddenly he was ashamed of himself. Mom *had* stood up to Stan. She probably *had* been goofy about him when he was little, the way Ken and Teresa were about Chris.

"Listen. Thanks a lot, okay?"

"Hon . . ."

"I gotta go. I'll tell Ms. Carmichael to send you the contracts. Bye."

The book. The book. He was going to get his book published!

He lay in his bed, too tired to sleep, too excited about the book again, too worried about Casey, who was supposed to ride the Star Runner in the jumper classes tomorrow.

He turned some Springsteen music on, low. Suddenly, and savagely, he missed his cat.

Chapter 11

He found out the difference between hunters and jumpers. Hunters were judged on form, smoothness, correct striding. Jumpers were judged on two things: getting over the jump and speed.

You didn't have to be real bright to figure out which was the most dangerous.

The jumper classes were the first ones the next morning. There were only seven riders entered; six of them were professional trainers. After the huge hunter classes of the day before—Jennifer's classes contained thirty riders—this seemed ominous to Travis. There weren't many who were good enough, or brave enough, to try this.

By seven he had fed, watered, and cleaned most of the stalls. He wandered over to the arena to watch the jump crew set up the course and got drafted into helping. He dragged poles around while distances and heights were measured and argued over.

These suckers were high. It was a funny thing, too, that when you were on a horse, the jumps seemed higher than when you were on the ground. He'd noticed that back at the barn, when Jennifer and Kelsey had talked him into riding— at a walk—around the arena. It amazed him how much bigger they seemed from a horse. He'd been scared the whole time he was riding that the horse would decide, suddenly and without warning, to jump.

"Casey riding this morning?" one of the jump crew asked. The crew were mostly fathers of the riders. "I heard she took a bad spill yesterday."

"Yeah," Travis said. "She's riding."

"That gray horse she's got, he's a mean one."

"Yeah, but if she ever gets him settled he'll be hard to beat," said someone else.

"He is a good-looking animal."

"I like that bay Jessie's got. Pretty *and* sane."

"Well, you know it was that jughead roan of Pete Wheeler's that won this class in the last show. Looks don't count here."

After the course was set, Travis went back to the stalls. The barn was relatively quiet—the show had lasted late last night and few people showed up to watch the first two classes. Casey had the Star Runner tied securely in the aisle, wiping him off with a polishing cloth. Braided, groomed, polished, his coat shining like heavy silver-gray silk, the Star Runner stood motionless, his dark eyes fixed on something only he could see. Parallel universe, thought Travis, suddenly remembering a term from his sci-fi stage. It was like the Star Runner's body was in one dimension and his mind in another.

Maybe he *was* an alien being, Travis thought, half joking, half not. After all, nobody said aliens *couldn't* be horses. Maybe that was why everyone was uneasy around him, why such a beautiful animal gave people the creeps. . . .

"Hey, kid." Casey tossed her cloth onto a lawn chair set up outside the tack stall. "Could you get me my saddle?"

"My name is Travis, not kid," he said, ticked off once too often by the way she referred to him. Two friggin' years difference in their age—it wasn't like she was old enough to be his mother.

"Sorry about that." She didn't sound sorry; but it wasn't until he was tightening the girth that he realized this was the first time she'd had anyone tack up for her.

"I bet you couldn't pick up your saddle," he accused her. "You did break some ribs yesterday."

She shrugged. "Naw, I just thought I'd get my money's worth out of you."

She checked the girth herself before she put on the bridle. Travis held the Star Runner, who was beginning to stamp and paw, while Casey changed from her navy-blue sweat jacket to her charcoal-gray riding coat, applied her lipstick quickly, without a mirror, and tucked her hair into her velvet hard-hat.

"Leg up, please." She stood beside the saddle and bent one leg back.

"You never needed a leg up before," he said, grabbing her boot and shoving her up. She could always jump straight up and catch the stirrup— Travis thought that was probably left over from her western riding days. He could picture that, Casey being a cowgirl. He could picture that real well.

"Stop being such a little mother—hen." She tapped him lightly on the head with her crop as she nudged the Star Runner into a walk.

"Get Sandman brushed," she called over her shoulder. "Jennifer's in the first flat class, and you know her."

The hell I will, Travis thought, and ran over to the schooling ring.

Casey walked the Star Runner around the ring twice in each direction, trotted him twice, cantered him collectedly in small circles.

"Boy, she's got him going well on the flat," said one of the girls watching from the bleachers. "Now if she could just keep him from going crazy jumping."

"Jesse says he'll never make a good jumper because he never listens in the ring."

Travis knew she meant "pays attention." Oh,

yeah, he thought. If he doesn't listen Casey'll just yell louder.

The Star Runner was snorting and blowing, almost panting, in rhythm with his strides. Casey put him over the practice jump once from either direction, then trotted out of the ring.

"Hey"—Travis ran up beside her where she stood by the entry gate—"is that all the warm-up you're going to do?"

Casey was looking at the course. "I thought I told you to groom Sandman."

"So fire me. Don't you need to school some more?" He moved over to miss the Star Runner's dancing hooves.

Casey's face was glowing. She was like a girl with the best date for the prom.

"Oh, I thought I'd surprise him a little this time. Open the gate for me, would you, ki—Travis?"

First one on the course, Travis thought wildly, swinging the gate open, doesn't even get to see how the jumps ride, damn her, and everybody thinks it's just the horse who's crazy.

"On course, the Star Runner, ridden by Casey Kencaide."

Travis wondered if she hadn't schooled more because it hurt too badly, and something about the way she sat up after the first jump convinced him he was right. Should have at least taped her ribs—the Star Runner threw a bucking fit in the corner, Casey got his head up and absolutely charged him at a five-foot vertical—he cleared it by a foot and the small crowd in the stands gasped. The next jump was a four-foot-high oxer with a four-foot spread; the Star Runner flattened out like a leaping cat to clear it. He shot up and down like a pogo stick through the final triple, and Casey had to make two finishing circles to get him back down to a trot.

Travis raced around to the exit gate, and it wasn't until he heard her laugh and say, "Well, we know it's jumpable," that he even thought about the fact that she'd gone clear—and if anyone else went clear she'd have to do it again, for speed.

"Well," he said. She winced a little as she slid off.

"Well what?" She was panting, like it hurt to breathe. "Here, cool him off a little while I watch the next couple of rounds."

"I'm going to get a nurse or something." He knew there was one around here somewhere.

"No," she said, "you're not."

She walked into a small cloud of congratulations around the entry gate, and Travis watched her until a sharp pain in his arm made him jump.

Goddamn horse had bitten him.

And it made Travis madder to realize he was afraid to retaliate, afraid to whack him across the nose with the reins like he would any other horse.

"Come on." He jerked the reins, careful not to get too close. His arm smarted from the bite—his leather jacket was all that had saved him from having a hunk of flesh ripped off. He walked the Star Runner up and down, listening to the cheers and groans of the crowd, as riders went clear or had a rail down.

More and more people were arriving, the place was filling up with screeching girls and harried mothers again.

"Travis! Travis!"

Jennifer and Kelsey came running up. "How'd Casey do?"

"She went clear."

They grabbed each other and jumped up and down, squealing like a couple of morons.

"Have they started the jump-off yet?"

"No, I think that's the last horse now."

And from the cheering it was another clear round.

"You better get tacked up," he said to Jennifer. She couldn't afford for Casey to get any madder—skipping last night's medal class in favor of piano recital had really ticked her off.

"I'm done!" Jennifer boasted. "He's clean and tacked and I'm dressed and ready."

"Oh," Kelsey said, giggling, "you're bleeding."

Travis looked down at his hand, not too surprised to see blood trickling out of his sleeve.

"I got bit."

"Boy, Casey *is* a grouch at the shows," Kelsey teased. Travis scowled at her. Some things weren't funny anymore.

Suddenly Casey was there, running the stirrups down.

"How many clear?"

"Three of us."

"When do you go?"

"First."

"Oh, Casey, no," Jennifer wailed.

Casey laughed. "Watch."

Travis boosted her up, and she trotted toward the schooling ring. She turned suddenly. "Jennifer, if you're late . . ."

The three of them ran to the stands to get a good place to watch.

"What's wrong with being first?" Travis asked. He was glad she was first, glad to get it over with.

"Oh, everything. You really have to go for time, since you don't know how anyone else will do—you don't get to watch anyone. Sometimes the last rider knows all she has to do is go clear—first, and you have to be clear *and* fast."

Travis stared unseeingly at the jump crew taking down the top rails of some of the jumps, raising some of the others. The jump-off course was shorter, tighter, higher.

"You know, I think she broke some ribs yesterday."

"That's nothing," said Kelsey. "Two years ago she rode all day with one arm in a cast and was reserve champion."

"The Star Runner, on course."

The Star Runner trotted sideways into the ring,

Casey holding him together like a coiled spring. Then the time buzzer sounded and the Star Runner shot forward like the head of a striking snake.

It was wrong, all wrong. Travis had been watching this stuff for weeks and nobody could jump at this speed, the horse would run right through the fences. Nobody could make those turns, pivoting two strides in front of the jumps, turning in mid-air like a cat, changing direction like a slammed tennis ball without slowing—

Casey, with the first visible effort Travis could catch, swung the Star Runner around just in time to keep him from jumping the exit gate.

She was through, it was over, and they hadn't touched a rail.

The crowd was frozen. Then Kelsey yelled, "Yea, Casey!" and a blast of applause boomed across the ring. Usually each barn cheered its own riders—this was the first time Travis had seen everyone in the stands on their feet clapping.

"Time for the Star Runner: nineteen point nine seven seconds."

Behind Travis a voice said, "That will teach me to ride against an ex–barrel racer."

Travis turned around, and the two remaining riders, a man in his early thirties, and a girl on a horse rumored to cost fifty thousand dollars, sat shaking their heads.

"Well, I'm going to save my neck, my horse, and my insurance," said the man. He did the course in twenty-six seconds with one rail down.

The girl made an effort—you could see it really amazed her to hear her time of twenty-three seconds. It wasn't until after her round that Travis realized he'd been gripping the arena rail so hard his hands were going numb.

"First place goes to the Star Runner, owned and ridden by Casey Kencaide," said the loudspeaker. Casey, on foot, trotted the Star Runner into the arena to pick up the ribbon and silver trophy. She took her prizes with a remote smile—a king of a conquering army accepting baubles, still reliving the battle.

Travis joined in the clapping, moving like a sleepwalker to the exit gate with the chattering girls.

"Casey, that was wonderful!"

"Congratulations!"

"Great, great ride!"

"Thanks." She smiled back at every compliment.

"Let me cool him off," begged Kelsey. Casey handed her the reins and she walked off with the gray as proudly as a groupie with a rock star.

"Go get Sandman warmed up while I change," Casey said to Jennifer. Travis held the ribbon and trophy while she pulled off her helmet. The hairnet went with it, and her hair, shining gold-on-brown, tumbled down her back. "Hurry."

Jennifer ran off. Travis followed Casey into the curtained tack stall, and after she'd shrugged out of her jacket he pinned her against the wall and kissed her. He had never said "I love you" to anyone in his life, but he was saying it now.

When he released her, she was staring into his eyes. Calmly. Not angry, not even halfway surprised.

"So what's all this about?"

"You know," he said, suddenly convinced she did know. There *was* something between them. Her upper arms in his hands were strong and warm; he desperately wanted all of her. Strong and warm and unafraid. . . .

Something like the polite mask she wore for the parents slid over her face.

"Jennifer's a sweet girl. I think she could schedule in a boyfriend."

"Don't," Travis said. It would kill him if she hid from him now. He was terrified that he'd blown everything. "You tell me there's nothing between us," he challenged.

"Okay," Casey said, "I like you. You're . . . brave."

"I killed the snake," Travis said, almost absently. She liked him. He hadn't even been convinced of that, only that there was this strange tie, bond, fate, between them.

"Snake, hell. Anyone could do that. You came down to the barn and helped me clean up that mess you made, when I never expected to see you again. You haven't been afraid to ask when you don't know things. . . . I like you a lot." She paused. "All day long people are asking me 'how?' and you come along, knowing why."

She slipped out of his grip, facing him levelly.

"But you saw what I just did. It wasn't being 'brave' for nineteen seconds. It was being brave a year ago when it took two people to hold him while I mounted. It was being brave enough to spend money I don't have on dressage lessons. It was all the time I spent riding instead of movies, pizza—and rolling around in the hay with a boyfriend. Can't you see that was more than just a jump-off? It was . . . it was . . ."

"It was art," said Travis.

Her eyes narrowed like Motorboat's in front of a mouse hole.

"How do you know this stuff? You know things about me my own mother doesn't know."

He just leaned forward and kissed her again, softly.

"With us, it'd be a lot more than a roll in the hay."

"I know," Casey answered. "That's what scares me."

He backed off, knowing if he pressed her he'd lose her.

The regret in her voice, saying no, thrilled him more than any yes he'd ever had.

Chapter 12

He did his first interview on television. It wasn't a big success. Ken's friend, Steve Slade, managed a local TV station and asked him to be on the noon news. Not a long interview, just a couple of minutes, nothing in depth. A piece of cake.

Travis said sure. He wasn't certain what in-depth was anyway; a couple of minutes shouldn't be too hard. He might as well start getting used to it.

Ken arranged to get him out of school for two hours, and drive him to the station.

"I've got to see a realtor anyway."

Travis was trying to figure out what he ought to wear; it took a long time for his mind to replay that last statement.

"What you going to see a realtor about?"

"I'm putting the place up for sale and looking for a house in town."

"What about Casey?" It popped into his head and it bounced right out of his mouth before he could stop it.

It certainly wasn't the first thing Ken expected him to ask. His eyebrows twisted upward.

"What about Casey?"

"Well," Travis said, "is she gonna have to get another barn or something?"

"Probably. I'll give her enough notice. Afraid of losing your job?"

Travis shrugged. He had thought of something else. He didn't know how to ask if there was going to be room for him in the new house.

"You won't mind changing schools?"

His neck muscles relaxed so suddenly he felt limp.

"Naw. I won't mind."

A new school. God, he'd love a crack at a new school. Maybe it'd be a bigger one with more different kinds of groups, he could find some people to hang out with and not be stuck playing the Invisible Man.

"Thanks," he said absently.

Ken didn't say, "For what?" He said, "You're welcome." So that saved a lot of embarrassing conversation.

"You want to sell the place?" Travis asked.

Ken sighed. "Kid, your mind travels in the strangest directions. Most people go from A to B to C—you go from A to maybe Q and end up at L. . . . I've got to sell it. I don't have the time or the capital to get into horse ranching, especially in this economy. I don't like to spend as much time driving as I'm doing. I think it'd be easier for Christopher if I were in town too."

"I thought maybe you guys were going to get back together."

"I don't know. You know what I dread? Dating. God, it used to be bad enough, asking 'What's your sign?' Now, it'll be 'How'd your blood test?' "

Travis shook his head. These old guys, they could think of the weirdest things. Dating.

"Aw, it'll be fun," he said, trying to cheer him up.

"You have no idea how much fun a Saturday night at home with your wife and kid and a pizza can be."

Travis sighed. The day a Saturday night home with a wife and kid and pizza looked fun to him, he was going to blow his brains out.

"Don't wear black," Ken said suddenly. "Steve told me to tell you not to wear black."

He wore his olive-colored long-sleeved buttoned undershirt, and when he realized how cold it was going to be here in the studio he left his jacket on too.

It was a big warehouse kind of room, the set was just a desk in front of a wall, a lot smaller than he'd thought it would be. There were cables lying around all over the floor. He tripped on two.

"Let's get you miked," Steve was saying. He'd introduced them to the newscaster, a young black woman who looked like a model, and the camera crew.

He sat behind the desk while they clipped a mike onto his collar, hiding the black wire under his jacket.

"Nervous?" asked Steve. He probably didn't leave his office for everybody they had on the noon news. He was taking the time because he was friends with Ken.

"Naw. If I goof up you can just shoot it again."

"What?"

"That's what we did in mass communications class. In sixth grade we taped a news show." Travis was growing uneasy, because this seemed to be a big joke to everyone.

"This is live," Steve said.

Travis felt his tongue starting to swell. It was a very weird sensation. It swelled until it felt as big as a dinner plate.

This was live.

"You were okay," Ken said. "You look good on camera."

Travis stared out the window. He hadn't been okay. He'd been god-awful. He must have looked like a moron. He'd been so nervous he'd actually gotten tears in his eyes—Ken said you couldn't tell, but Travis knew he'd still looked like a moron. A good-looking moron, maybe.

"You just have to learn to speak in sentences, you know, answer questions with more than yeah and naw. Get glib."

Get glib.

"On TV, you don't have time for a lot of pauses. Every second seems like a minute, a minute seems like an hour. You've got to remember your medium."

"So who made you a director?" Travis muttered. Who the hell cared? His medium was writing, not talking.

He wanted to do this, interviews and stuff. For the first time he realized how bad he wanted to do this.

I can learn it, he thought. Next time'll be different. In his mind he started writing answers to the questions she'd asked him. Writing answers in sentences. Getting glib.

He'd hoped maybe one of the teachers would ask him where he'd been that morning; he would be casual as hell while replying, "Oh, I was on the news," or maybe, "Doing a television show." He was getting a little antsy to let them know they were dealing with a real writer here.

But nobody asked him anything. Everyone had left him alone and now they thought he wanted it that way. They had made him into a loner and then acted like it was his idea. Travis had never before realized how much your status depended on other people. He'd thought you got to choose your group. Well, you didn't. But he tried to pull off the loner role with as much dignity as possible: When the guys in the smoke hole talked about going to the river to do some long-neckin' (he had picked up on some of the local jargon: long-neckin' meant drinking beer) he didn't beg to go too. Bunch of hicks in a four-wheel drive, sitting in the sand chugging Coors—how cool could that be?

He walked off to spend his lunch hour in the library. If they got the impression he was some kind of psycho who'd come to school with a gun someday, well, that was their impression.

He wanted out of this school so bad. Even if it meant not seeing Casey every day. He had to get out of here before he broke down and begged to go long-neckin' with hicks.

When he answered the phone that afternoon he wasn't too surprised that it was Joe. He'd been thinking about the guys so strong, he'd even had a feeling that it was Joe when the phone rang. Sometimes he was kind of psychic about phone calls and stuff like that.

"Travis?"

"Yeah. Joe?"

"Yeah. Can you come and get me?"

"I can't hear you, man. This is a lousy connection."

"I'm at the Quik Trip over on Highway Fifty-one. Can you come and get me? I can't walk, man,

I jumped outta the car and messed up my leg. . . ."

Travis could hardly understand him, his voice had no air behind it, he was surprised now he'd recognized it—what the hell was going on?

"How'd you get here?"

"I hitched, man, and I had to jump outta the last car, the guy was getting weird with me, I guess I better get used to that. . . ."

It sounded like Joe was sobbing. Or maybe just too tired to even talk. Something was really wrong.

"What's up?"

"It's bad, Travis. Really bad. Can you come and get me?"

"I don't have any wheels, man. My uncle won't be home for hours."

"Oh, don't tell your uncle. Don't tell anybody, man."

"Hold on."

Travis ran to the kitchen window. Casey's Jeep was parked by the barn.

"Listen, I think I can get there." He paused. "How bad?"

"The twins are dead." Joe's voice sounded flat. Flat and old.

"Orson killed them. And I helped him."

Travis felt so spacey. For a second he thought he was going to drop the phone. He didn't ask if this was some kind of sick joke.

"Stay there. I'll get a ride."

"Okay," Joe said, and hung up.

"I need to borrow your Jeep."

Casey looked up from her record books. I don't think—what's wrong?"

"Just for a couple of minutes—to go to the Quik Trip."

"Hey, this is some nicotine fit."

Travis wanted to smack her across the room, but she said quickly, "What is it?"

"I need to pick up a guy at the Quik Trip, he hitched this far, it's real important—you drive if you want, but let's go, okay?"

She got to her feet, looking at her watch. "I've got a lesson . . . what the hell, they've been late for me—"

She drove even fast enough to suit him, raced down to the highway like she did across the fields, chasing the Star Runner. Travis gripped his seat, too scared to think. He could think later, when Joe told him what had happened—the twins dead?

He could remember the last time he'd seen them, the night before his big fight with Stan, they were working on the Trans Am, he was sitting on the washing machine in their garage watching them, drinking Pepsi because their mom was home. He remembered how pale they looked under garage light, skinny, Mike under the hood and Billy laughing at whatever Travis was saying. He'd been lying extravagantly about something, he couldn't remember what, they wouldn't allow smoking in the garage, they thought they were such hotshot mechanics. . . .

Joe was sitting on the curb in front of the Quik Trip. He almost fell as he got up, and limped to the Jeep. To Travis he seemed like someone stumbling in his sleep, exhausted by a nightmare he couldn't awake from. Travis was stunned. Joe was thinner, dirtier, and older. And he knew these changes were recent—for the first time he could believe stories he'd heard about people turning gray overnight.

He jumped out of the Jeep to help him. Joe yelped when he grabbed his arm.

"Sorry, man," he muttered, heaving himself into the front seat. "I think I tore some muscles or somethin'."

He gazed at Casey.

"She's cool," Travis said, hopping in back, and Casey proved it by not asking any questions, just speeding back to the barn.

In Travis's room Joe stretched out on the bed, not even taking his shoes off, staring straight up at the ceiling. Travis couldn't figure out what to do. In a little while Joe started shaking, and tears ran down his face, but he didn't even seem to notice, like this had happened so much he was used to it.

Travis went to the kitchen and poured out a couple of good shots of bourbon and dropped a handful of ice cubes in it. He'd worry about Ken later.

Joe pulled himself up into a half-sitting position, leaning back against the headboard. He gulped the bourbon like it was water—Travis realized he should have brought water to begin with, but Joe did quit shaking so much.

"Got anything to eat?"

Travis doubted it—he came up with a couple of cold weenies in stale buns, but Joe ate them without complaint, slowly, not bothering to wipe the streaking tears off his face.

"So what happened?" Travis asked finally. He dreaded knowing.

"The twins are dead."

"Yeah. So how?"

"Orson killed them. Took a twenty-two, oh, God—"

Joe finished off his bourbon.

"He tried to make me shoot Mike, but I wouldn't. You think that might help, at my trial, that I didn't pull the trigger? I thought he was ready to kill me, too, and he still couldn't make me—"

"Start from the start," Travis said.

Joe munched along on his hot dog, obviously rewinding his story in his mind, trying to decide where "start" was.

"We've been working for Orson," he said—he meant himself and the twins, he wasn't used to the fact that they were past tense yet. "I wrote you that, or told you, right?"

Travis nodded.

"It wasn't dope," Joe said. He didn't seem to

know what to say next. "We were doing houses. . . ."

Doing houses? thought Travis. Painting or something? He couldn't imagine Orson organizing house painting, or why it would cause him to kill someone. But he just let Joe work on his second bourbon, because he was remembering vividly how it felt to be scared like that.

"Robbing houses. Orson would scout neighborhoods and me and the twins would break into the houses he picked, you know how good they are with tools and stuff, it wasn't too hard, a lot of times I just stood lookout because they could get in small windows, we just took easy stuff, you know, Orson fenced it, he said people's insurance covered it, nobody was really getting hurt, and he paid us, you know, like for each job. If we got a lot of stuff it was more. He knew how to get rid of the stuff, so we just took whatever he gave us."

Joe closed his eyes and sighed. Travis was sick with cold apprehension. Joe was in big, big trouble. And even in the middle of his terror for his friend came the selfish, unbidden thought: Thank God it's not me!

"I quit," Joe said. "You think they'll believe me when I tell 'em I quit?"

His sad olive-brown eyes fixed on Travis, desperate for hope, but Travis couldn't even nod.

"We did this one house, we thought it was empty, but just as we were packing up the silver this old lady came in and started screeching—

Billy shoved her and she fell, we ran out of there, she wasn't hurt because it was in the papers, but I got to thinkin' about Grandma, what if somebody shoved her, old ladies break bones real easy, you know. And I didn't want to do this anymore and I quit. The twins said they quit too." He sighed. "But they didn't. They did one more job and didn't tell Orson."

Travis's mind raced around and around. Ken could help him, he knew the law, he could . . . And at the same time he told himself over and over, it couldn't have happened to *him*. Oh, no. Suppose he had stayed at home, had been hanging out with them, he'd never have done anything so dumb. Robbing houses and . . . He'd never have been so dumb.

He stared at Joe and thought of all the reasons why it wouldn't have happened to *him*.

"Orson came by and got me. He said he'd heard the twins pulled a job without cutting him in. I think they found a different fence, I don't know, I quit and I thought they did too. Orson said he was going to kick ass. That's all I thought he was going to do, honest, he said he was going to do a little ass kickin' and teach them a lesson. He'd been drinkin' and smoking grass and coke too. I was scared to get out of the van—he wasn't mad at me and I was trying to keep it like that. The twins were hanging out in the parking lot by the park and Orson got out and got them and they just climbed in; we've been doing more grass

since you left, Travis, it's easier to get than booze.
They were pretty stoned. And all the way up the
mountain, he was driving up the mountain road,
toward the reservoir, we kept drinking and smoking and it was like a foggy bad dream, like you
can't wake up from, Orson ranting on and on
about how they double-crossed him, how he was
going to fix them. It was scaring me, man, but it
was like it wasn't happening either. It just wasn't
real. You ever have something happen, and it just
didn't seem real?''

Travis nodded. He knew Orson's van. He could
picture everything, the black night out the windows, the heavy smell of the grass, the glare of the
dashboard lights on Orson's mad face. Crazy
mad, drunk and stoned.

He pictured the silent twins, passing a bottle
back and forth. It wouldn't seem real to them
either.

"Anyway, Orson drove down one of those side
roads, a dirt one, it was too bouncy to drink. Then
he stopped and got out and rolled the side door
open and made them get out. And me too. They
ended up sitting on a log, Orson was still yelling
and I was too scared to sit down with them. And
he was waving a gun around. I thought it was just
to scare them. I thought that right up to when he
shot Billy in the head and he went over backward.
Mike just sat there, staring at the ground. Orson
said to me, 'You do this one,' but I wouldn't. I
didn't say anything but I wouldn't. Then he was

yelling, 'Look at me, damn you,' at Mike, but he kept staring at the ground, shaking his head. Orson shot him too. I thought I was next, but he drove me back to town, saying I knew better than to tell anyone.

"I got a bus to St. Louis and then hitched the rest of the way—the last guy got a little weird with me and I jumped out of the car. . . .

"You know what I keep thinking about? Leaving them up there on the mountain, it was a real cold night and they didn't have jackets. . . ."

Joe started shaking so his ice cubes rattled.

Travis finally said, "You sure they were dead?"

Joe nodded.

"When did this happen?"

"I think it was two nights ago, I ain't sure anymore."

Travis found himself shaking. But it wouldn't happen to me, he kept thinking. I'd have jumped out of the van, grabbed the gun, knocked Orson out . . . He kept running it over in his mind, changing the story, fixing it.

Fixing everything.

Chapter 13

It crossed Travis's mind to try to hide all this from
Ken, but he soon realized that wouldn't work. For
one thing, Joe sacked out into a sleep that resem-
bled a coma, and Travis would have to take Christopher's bed; but mostly Travis wanted somebody
else to lay this on—he wanted help.

What was going to happen to Joe? He tried to
keep that question at the top of his mind, but if he
let down his guard for a second, he found himself
dwelling on how close he had come to being in
the same mess.

If he had hit Stan just a little bit harder . . .

Ken took it a lot more calmly than Travis had
expected. They stayed up till two o'clock talking
about it—at least they ended up talking. At first
Travis tried to persuade him to get Joe on a plane

out of the country. When Ken refused even to discuss that option Travis got a little wild, but by midnight he was worn out and facing facts. Ken was going to call the authorities first thing in the morning; he was going to do all that was legally possible; he was going to help find a good lawyer. Joe was going back.

It was settled and Travis had known all along this was how it was going to be settled and he didn't think Joe was going to be too surprised.

He wasn't. Travis finally had to go shake him awake the next morning; he ate his toast and drank his coffee and listened to the plans with dull indifference. Travis remembered when he'd worked for the vet: a couple of times people brought in dogs that had been hit by a car—they had the same look.

And Joe was tired. He was too tired to think of showering, but Travis made him, and ran his clothes through the washer and dryer. It might be his last private shower for a while.

For some reason that thought made Travis cry. He leaned on the washer and cried. The machine was noisy, nobody could hear him.

Joe was ready at last. He seemed to be walking in his sleep. Travis couldn't help remembering the bouncing bravado he'd managed himself, when the cops came for *him*, but then Stan hadn't been a friend, or really dead. He let Joe sit up front, even though he hated being scrunched up in the back.

"What's that?" Joe sat up and looked around, like someone trying to wake up.

"Thunder," Travis said.

"We're under a severe thunderstorm watch," Ken said. It seemed like a last-ditch effort for a normal conversation; they were reduced to talking about the weather.

"Does that mean like tornadoes and stuff?"

"Naw." Travis reassured him with the line he'd heard: "Not this time of year."

"I don't know," Ken said absentmindedly. "A few years ago we had one on Christmas."

Now he tells me, Travis thought. Actually, he hadn't really noticed the dark gray sky, it seemed such a natural extension of how everything was going—he would have been shocked and depressed by blazing sunshine this morning. The distant zigzag flashes through the blacker clouds to the west were like his thoughts, racing across his mind, the growing thunder like the march of doom.

Nobody tried to talk again. It was over quickly. They were in some building. It didn't seem like a police station, but there were policemen waiting to take Joe, men in suits to talk to Ken—Travis tried to take notes in his mind but everything blurred. Everything but the quick hug he gave Joe.

He was shaking.

"So what's going to happen?" he asked, finally breaking silence on the way home. The lightning was closer now, crackling like skeleton fingers across the sky, the thunder booming and rolling (giants bowling, he remembered from when he was little, he'd thought thunder was giants bowling—had he thought that up or had he seen it in a cartoon a long time ago?). But it wasn't raining yet. The hairs on his arms, on the back of his neck, stood and wiggled.

"Do I look like God?" Ken said. "How should I know?"

Not much, Travis thought, not with those bags under your eyes.

"I mean *legally.*"

"Sorry. Legally. Well, it depends on whether or not they catch this other guy. How much of his story is corroborated by the evidence. And a big factor is whether he's tried as a juvenile or an adult. How old is he?"

"Sixteen," Travis said, then remembered, with a sinking feeling, that Joe's mom had held him back a year, before grade school. Joe was the only person he knew who'd flunked kindergarten. "Seventeen."

"It could go either way."

Travis stared out at the trees dancing in the wind.

"It wouldn't have happened if I'd been there," he burst out. "I never liked that scuzz-ball Orson. I'd never have let them get suckered into working for him—if I'd stayed home this wouldn't have happened."

"Maybe something else would've happened," Ken said. Maybe it would have been you and your stepdad murdering each other. Fate and will—it's baffled better minds than mine." In a minute he added, "Fate's what happens to you, and will is what you *make* happen to you."

Travis just nodded, thinking, Geez, does he think I'm a moron?

"You know," Ken said slowly, "I've got a friend who just got out of a Spanish prison a few years ago. He was in for twelve years, for five ounces of hash. And it could have just as easily been me. He's still in Spain, bartending. He didn't exactly pick up marketable skills in there. Why him and not me?"

"You used to do hash too?" Travis was shocked beyond belief. Sure, he knew adults smoked; the twins' stepfather had always shared his stash with them. Straight-arrow Ken? Never.

"What do you think—your generation invented sex, drugs, and rock and roll?"

Travis was quiet. Well, we've perfected it, he thought.

"We were in Spain at the same time, he came over on the freighter with me and Teresa—he tried to cross the French border, holding—we chickened out at the last minute. . . . Here is old Achilles, kid, to tell you: You are not going to believe you were ever that dumb. Goddamn!" A bolt of lightning struck so close they heard the sizzle; the immediate thunder boom rattled the car.

Will and fate—he could will himself into writing a book, it was fate that got the right person to read it. Fate had kept him from one murder, God knows, at the time he'd meant to kill Stan: he was sure will would have kept him out of this one. What was it in the end? Which one had the biggest say in your life?

A gust of wind pushed at the car.

"You sure this isn't a tornado?" Travis gripped the dashboard.

"I'm not positive. I just hope we don't get caught in a flash flood."

Flash flood. Great. Like there weren't enough complications in life with people—nature had to get its two cents in.

"She's filed," Ken said suddenly.

"What?"

"Teresa. She's going ahead with it."

Travis looked at Ken's drawn face. Maybe this was why he'd been so detached through Joe's ordeal, why he hadn't bothered to give Travis a be-careful-how-you-choose-your-friends lecture (although, at this point, Travis was having doubts he'd ever meant to—apparently some of Ken's friends weren't upstanding citizens either).

"You know what's one of the worst things about this? It's humiliating—it puts us in the same class as all the other jerks divorcing. I thought we were better than that."

"I thought maybe you guys were going to get back together."

Travis was thinking about the time Teresa'd spent the night. He'd been so sure it was a good sign.

"I thought so too. Maybe."

A crackling fork of lightning lit a black cloud. It was incredible how far up that cloud went, like a tower. There was so much energy coming off this storm, it was more exhilarating than scary.

"What did you mean, that time you said, 'It all started with the Cuisinart'?"

Ken gave a short laugh. "I'm sure it started long before that, but at the time, the Cuisinart got me to thinking, Now, what the hell does she need that thing for? Cooking is not Teresa's favorite pastime. Then I started thinking: Now, why did we buy an old farmhouse and redo it to look like a redone old farmhouse? I'd very carefully research cars, twelve years ago, to see what the best was. You know what I got? A BMW. I got rid of the thing last year, same time I got rid of the horses. But even as far back as college, the year Teresa and I backpacked around Europe, every goddamn college kid in America was backpacking around Europe."

Ken, thought Travis, you are not making sense. He really hoped ol' Ken wasn't cracking up.

"Then we took up skiing. And skiing was on the cover of *Time*. And suddenly I knew what Brie was, and then Teresa, who doesn't have a sweet tooth, developed a taste for chocolate. Just the same time Brie and chocolate swept the nation. I'm sick of feeling like a lemming. I'm sick of *stuff*."

"So, what does Teresa say?"

"She says let's enjoy a few things. She says, 'You hate your job, get another one!' She says she's too old to sleep on sidewalks."

"You going to get another job?"

Travis was trying to make some sense out of all this, and he wondered if Teresa felt the same way. She was the sensible one, it seemed to him.

"Another job? In this economy? I'm lucky to have a job. I have to think about Christopher— that's another thing. I used to always say I'd never send my kid to a private school unless I could guarantee him a private life, but now, what's going on in the public school system scares the hell out of me."

Hell, he'll live through it, Travis thought, but then, why not a private school if that'd be better?

"I think you're really messing up, man," Travis said.

"I probably am," Ken agreed. "It won't be the first time."

"Yeah, but it'll be the worst. Was my old man this stubborn?"

Ken laughed. "You think that's it, I'm just being stubborn?"

"I don't know what you're being but, geez, man, you want to keep Teresa and Chris, do something!"

Ken tightened his grip on the wheel as the car swayed in the wind. "Well, it's a lot more complicated."

Oh, sure. That was a good excuse for not making a move. Travis promised himself, he swore, he'd always make a move. Even if it was the wrong move, at least he'd know he did something besides balk like a mule and mutter "complicated."

As they pulled into the drive, they could see Casey racing around, trying to catch Sandman in the paddock. The rest of the paddocks were empty, except the one where the Star Runner was plunging and bowing, whirling and charging.

Why didn't she get him in first? Travis thought. He's going to jump out in a second. Then he knew: Of course, she'd look out for everyone else's horse first.

They both jumped out of the car—Travis had a hard time getting his door shut against the wind. The temperature was dropping rapidly. It was almost as dark as dusk, except for the weird strobing effect of the lightning.

"Don't touch the railing!" Ken yelled at him, then threw the gate open and ran to grab Sandman's lead rope from Casey.

"I'll get him in! Get the Star Runner!"

For a second Travis was surprised to see how easily Ken handled the nervous horse. Then he remembered: That was what Ken had wanted to do with his life, raise horses. He hadn't ever seen Ken near one. . . .

There was a ripping sound, the sky splitting, and a finger of light touched the pecan tree at the back of the house. A crack and an explosion that deafened him.

This was death dancing around him in the skies, and for a second Travis wanted to run; then he broke loose from fear into a kind of crazy exhilaration. The Star Runner covered the paddock in one leap and took the five-foot railing in the next. Travis felt what it was that Casey felt: the Star Runner, to tame that Star Runner, it would be conquering worlds. . . .

The railing was humming. The steel poles were vibrating and pulsating with energy. Don't touch it, Travis thought, it's death. He turned and jumped into the Jeep with Casey, he'd been aware of her, the sky, the storm, the battlefield play of earth and air, all at the same time. Their eyes locked for just a second, and they laughed out loud at the same time. . . .

He seemed to hear Ken calling out, warning, but he was far behind now, they were racing like the wind, the earth was moving like a live thing under the wheels, the whole landscape was changed, charged, a different color, nothing familiar except that dark racing figure ahead.

The pasture gate was leaning, nearly flattened by the wind, and they charged on across it without stopping. They could gain on the Star Runner here, a long flat stretch except for the gullies that nearly threw them from the Jeep. They were gaining now, not chasing him, joining him.

Travis looked at Casey laughing into the wind and thought: I'll remember that profile to the day I die. No matter how it works for us later, I'll always have this. . . .

The sky opened, lit to the ceiling, a light brighter than he could ever have imagined, showing huge towers and spires reaching to heaven—

He lay tasting dirt and aching and wondering at the stillness. The wind still tore across the land, the sky was still flashing, but it was quiet as a tomb.

He wondered if he was dead, then decided he hurt too much to be dead. He felt sad, as if he'd been awakened from a wonderful dream.

Casey! He pushed himself up and looked around wildly. The Jeep lay overturned in a small gulley. But then something stirred just a few feet away, and Casey slowly forced her way to her feet. He, too, got up. The center of the storm was farther away now, flashing behind them. He felt a few pelts of water. He limped up to stand beside her and she took his hand, winding her fingers in his.

No heat, no passion, just gratitude for a human touch.

"What is it?" he said. He realized then that he was deaf. And it didn't shock him like the desolation of her face.

There was nothing. Just the windswept pasture, the overturned Jeep, and the line of trees. The acrid smell of electricity, the smell of something burning . . . flesh burning.

Nothing. He gazed at the empty pasture.

It was raining now, harder. It felt like tears, it felt like blood, on his face.

Chapter 14

Travis lay on his bed, going over his manuscript. He was absentmindedly correcting things, the technical stuff mostly, cutting description, fiddling with a comma, trying to figure out how to let people know what a character was saying without writing word for word what he was saying. "He swore" worked pretty good, but he needed something else too. . . .

He turned down the music.

Through the open window he could hear the mockingbirds fighting over what was left of the pecan tree. He rolled off the bed and pulled his desk chair to the window.

The revisions were beginning to bore him, now that the novelty of the editor's marks had worn off. The book was okay, and the reality of publication *(it was really going to happen!)* could still stop his breath, but he wasn't living this book anymore. He just wanted it done.

He listened to the birds. He had a great appreciation of the sense of hearing now, after being stone deaf for two days and panicked that it might be forever.

He folded his arms on the windowsill and rested his chin on them.

Spring wasn't bad. Fall was always his favorite time of year, but spring wasn't bad at all.

There was the realtor, in her navy suit and plasticized hair, showing someone around the property. The economy was bad, it was a bad time to be selling, but every once in a while someone came to look.

He had to keep his room straighter.

Teresa had filed for divorce, but now she was dragging her heels about going through with it. Christopher had started bed-wetting and both Ken and Teresa seemed unduly freaked out about it. Travis thought if it'd bring them together again he'd personally load Chris up with juice every night. And a couple of nights he had.

He was tired of their story and wished for a happy ending.

But now he thought stories didn't have endings, only pausing places.

Joe's story was still stuck on whether he was an adult or a juvenile, but Orson was going to get to sit on death row while his ending was being debated.

It was funny, the thought of what might have been, had he stayed—"what if?"—could still make Travis sick with dread. But the memory of the storm, of racing lightning, when he had been so close to death he could have reached out to touch it—that only brought an odd kind of joy.

Faintly, he could hear Casey yelling, "Heels. Heels! Heels!" He smiled. They were good friends now, close in a real funny way, free to fuss at each other, or laugh when no one else got the joke; she only had to raise an eyebrow to let him know what she was thinking, and sometimes she seemed to read his mind. They had a deal together, to quit smoking.

But something was gone. The intensity of a flaming candle, a laugh in the face of danger. He tried to remember the heat he had felt for her before, but it was fading now, like the memory of the storm, like the memory of the Star Runner, who, after all, had been just a horse.

Casey was still a good trainer. She still did well at the shows, she had a waiting list of people who wanted to ride with her. But there was something missing . . . he still loved her, but not the same way.

But he couldn't, wouldn't, believe that he missed the horse.

He could hear the realtor, in the house now, chirping about moldings, whatever they were.

He didn't much care about the place selling—Casey had already found another barn—except maybe it would cheer Ken up. Ken had promised him he could transfer to East River High, and it looked like he'd get to start with summer school, since he was flunking English. (This was going to be great in interviews, he thought. "The year I sold my book I flunked English." Ha!)

He would be in classes with Jennifer. He had gone with her and some of her friends to get pizza, to movies, they were a little preppy for him but he could get along with them. He had never felt so protective of anyone as he did of Jennifer.

He looked at his manuscript. It was just a stack of paper, pretty soon to be a book, but it wasn't the whole world anymore. Nell (he could call her Nell now) was nagging him to begin another one right away, so he'd have a good start on it before this one came out.

"Get going now," she warned him, "or you'll freak at the reality of the audience, once reviews come in."

Yeah, yeah, sure, Travis thought. But anyway, he did have an idea. . . .

He pulled his chair up to the desk and rolled a blank piece of paper into his typewriter.

He sat there, waiting.

About the Author

S. E. Hinton wrote her first novel, *The Outsiders,* when she was sixteen. It and three others *(That Was Then, This Is Now; Rumble Fish;* and *Tex)* were all made into major motion pictures.

S. E. Hinton lives in Tulsa, Oklahoma.

ML